Jacqueline Wilson's

FUNNY GIRLS

Jacqueline Wilson's

FUNNY GIRLS

THE STORY OF TRACY BEAKER and
THE BED AND BREAKFAST STAR

Illustrated by Nick Sharratt

CORGI YEARLING

JACQUELINE WILSON'S FUNNY GIRLS
A CORGI YEARLING BOOK 978 0 440 87022 7

THE STORY OF TRACY BEAKER
First published in Great Britain by Doubleday
Text copyright © Jacqueline Wilson, 1991
Illustrations copyright © Nick Sharratt, 1991

THE BED AND BREAKFAST STAR
First published in Great Britain by Doubleday
Text copyright © Jacqueline Wilson, 1994
Illustrations copyright © Nick Sharratt, 1994

This collection first published as
THE JACQUELINE WILSON COLLECTION in 1997 by Corgi Yearling,
an imprint of Random House Children's Publishers UK,
A Random House Group Company

This edition published 2012

3 5 7 9 10 8 6 4 2

Text in this edition copyright © Jacqueline Wilson, 1997
Illustrations in this edition copyright © Nick Sharratt, 1997

Penguin Random House is committed to a sustainable future for
our business, our readers and our planet. This book is made from
Forest Stewardship Council® certified paper.

MIX
Paper from
responsible sources
FSC® C018179

Printed and bound in Great Britain by Clays Ltd, St Ives plc

Set in New Century Schoolbook LT

Corgi Yearling Books are published by Random House Children's Publishers UK,
61–63 Uxbridge Road, London W5 5SA

www.randomhousechildrens.co.uk
www.randomhouse.co.uk
www.totallyrandombooks.co.uk

Addresses for companies within The Random House Group Limited can be found at:
www.randomhouse.co.uk/offices.htm

THE RANDOM HOUSE GROUP Limited Reg. No. 954009

A CIP catalogue record for this book is available from the British Library.

BY JACQUELINE WILSON

ILLUSTRATED BY NICK SHARRATT

CORGI YEARLING BOOKS

To Bryony, David, Miranda,
Jason and Ryan

ABOUT ME

My name is Tracy Beaker

I am 10 **years** 2 **months old**.

My birthday is on 8 May. It's not fair, because that dopey Peter Ingham has his birthday then too, so we just got the one cake between us. And we had to hold the knife to cut the cake together. Which meant we only had half a wish each. Wishing is for babies anyway. They don't come true.

I was born at some hospital somewhere. I looked cute when I was a little baby but I bet I yelled a lot.

I am cms tall. I don't know. I've tried measuring with a ruler but it keeps wobbling about and I can't reach properly. I don't want to get any of the other children to help me. This is my private book.

I weigh kgs. I don't know that either. Jenny has got scales in her bathroom but they're stones and pounds. I don't weigh many of them. I'm a little titch.

My eyes are black and I can make them go all wicked and witchy. I quite fancy being a witch. I'd make up all these incredibly evil spells and wave my wand and ZAP Louise's golden curls would all fall out and ZAP Peter Ingham's silly squeaky voice would get sillier and squeakier and he'd grow whiskers and a long tail and ZAP . . . there's not room on this bit of the page, but I've still got all sorts of ZAPs inside my head.

8

My hair is fair and very long and curly. I am telling fibs. It's dark and difficult and it sticks up in all the wrong places.

My skin is spotty when I eat a lot of sweets.

Stick a photo of yourself here

I'm not really cross-eyed. I was just pulling a silly face.

I **started this book on** I don't know. Who cares what the date is? You always have to put the date at school. I got fed up with this and put 2091 in my Day Book and wrote about all these rockets and space ships and monsters legging it down from Mars to eat us all up, as if we'd all whizzed one hundred years into the future. Miss Brown didn't half get narked.

MORE THINGS ABOUT ME

Things I like

My lucky number is 7. So why didn't I get fostered by some fantastic rich family when I was seven then?

My favourite colour is blood red, so watch out, ha-ha.

My best friend is　Well, I've had heaps and heaps, but Louise has gone off with Justine and now I haven't got anyone just at the moment.

I like eating　everything. I like birthday cake best. And any other kind of cake. And Smarties and Mars Bars and big buckets of popcorn and jelly spiders and Cornettos and Big Macs with french fries and strawberry milk shakes.

My favourite name is　Camilla. There was a lovely little baby at this other home and that was her name. She was a really sweet kid with fantastic hair that I used to try to get into loads of little plaits and it must have hurt her sometimes but she never cried. She really liked me, little Camilla. She got fostered quick as a wink. I begged her foster mum and dad to bring her back to see me but they never did.

11

I like drinking pints of bitter. That's a joke. I *have* had a sip of lager once but I didn't like it.

My favourite game is playing with make-up. Louise and I once borrowed some from Adele who's got heaps. Louise was a bit boring and just tried to make herself look beautiful. I turned myself into an incredible vampire with evil shadowy eyes and blood dribbling down my chin. I didn't half scare the little ones.

My favourite animal is Well, there's a rabbit called Lettuce at this home but it's a bit limp, like its name. It doesn't sit up and give you a friendly lick like a dog. I think I'd like a Rottweiler – and then all my enemies had better WATCH OUT.

My favourite TV programme is
horror films.

Best of all I like   being with my
mum.

Things I don't like

the name   Justine. Louise. Peter.
Oh there's heaps and heaps of names
I can't stand.

eating   stew. Especially when it's
got great fatty lumps in it. I used to
have this horrid foster mother called
Aunty Peggy and she was an awful
cook. She used to make this slimy stew
like molten sick and we were supposed
to eat it all up, every single bit. Yuck.

Most of all I hate   Justine. That
Monster Gorilla. And not seeing my
mum.

MY OWN FAMILY

Stick a photo of you and your family here

This was when I was a baby. See, I was sweet then. And this is my mum. She's ever so pretty. I wish I looked more like her.

The people in my own family are My mum. I don't have a dad. I lived with my mum when I was little and we got on great but then she got this Monster Gorilla Boyfriend and I hated him and he hated me back and beat me up and so I had to be taken into care. No wonder my mum sent him packing.

My own family live at I'm not sure exactly where my mum lives now because she has to keep moving about because she gets fed up living in one place for long.

The phone number is Well, I don't know, do I? Funny though, I always used to bag this toy telephone in the playhouse at school and pretend I was phoning my mum. I used to have these long long conversations with her. They were just pretend of course, but I was only about five then and sometimes it got to be quite real.

Things about my family that I like I like my mum because she's pretty and good fun and she brings me lovely presents.

MY FOSTER FAMILY

There's no point filling this bit in. I haven't got a foster family at the moment.

I've had two. There was Aunty Peggy and Uncle Sid first of all. I didn't like them much and I didn't get on with the other kids so I didn't care when they got rid of me. I was in a children's home for a while and then I had this other couple. Julie and Ted. They were young and friendly and they bought me a bike and I thought it was all going to be great and I went to live with them and I was ever so good and did everything they said and I thought I'd be staying with them until my mum came to get me for good but then . . . I don't want to write about it. It ended up with me getting turfed out THROUGH NO FAULT OF MY OWN. I was so mad I smashed up the bike so I don't even have that any more. And now I'm in a new children's home and they've advertised me in the papers but there weren't many takers and now I think they're getting a bit desperate. I don't care though. I expect my mum will come soon anyway.

MY SCHOOL

My school is called   It's Kinglea Junior School. I've been to three other schools already. This one's OK I suppose.

My teacher is called Miss Brown. She gets cross if we just call her Miss.

Subjects I do Story-writing. Arithmetic. Games. Art. All sorts of things. And we do Projects only I never have the right stuff at the Home so I can't do it properly and get a star.

I like Story-writing best. I've written heaps of stories, and I do pictures for them too. I make some of them into books. I made Camilla a special baby book with big printed words and pictures of all the things she liked best, things like TEDDY and ICE-CREAM and YOUR SPECIAL FRIEND TRACY.

I also like Art. We use poster paints. We've got them at the Home too but they get all gungy and mucked up and the brushes are useless. They've got good ones at school. This is a painting I did yesterday. If I was a teacher I'd give it a gold star. *Two* gold stars.

19

My class is   3a.

People in my class   I can't list all their names, I'd be here all night. I don't know some of them yet. There's not much point making friends because I expect I'll be moving on soon.

Other teachers   Oh, they're all boring. Who wants to write about them?

I get to school by   going in the Minibus. That's how all the kids in the home get to school. I'd sooner go in a proper car or walk it by myself but you're not allowed.

It takes   hours   mins
It varies. Sometimes it takes ages because the little kids can't find their pencil cases and the big ones try to bunk off and we just have to hang about waiting.

Things I don't like about school

They all wear grey things, that's the uniform, and I've only got navy things from my last school. The teachers know why and I don't get into trouble but the other kids stare.

BEING IN CARE

My social worker is called Elaine and sometimes she's a right pain, haha.

We talk about all sorts of boring things.

But I don't like talking about my mum. Not to Elaine. What I think about my mum is private.

older, I would live in this really great modern house all on my own, and I'd have my own huge bedroom with all my own things, special bunk beds just for me so that I'd always get the top one and a Mickey Mouse alarm clock like Justine's and my own giant set of poster paints and I'd have some felt tips as well and no-one would ever get to borrow them and mess them up and I'd have my own television and choose exactly what programmes I want, and I'd stay up till gone twelve every night and I'd eat at McDonald's every single day and I'd have a big fast car so I could whizz off and visit my mum whenever I wanted.

a policeman, I would arrest the Monster Gorilla and I'd lock him up in prison for ever.

a kitten, I would grow very long claws and sharp teeth and scratch and bite everyone so they'd get really scared of me and do everything I say.

yelled at, I would yell back.

invisible, I would spy on people.

very tall, I would stamp on people with my great big feet.

very rich, I would buy my own house and then ... I've done all that bit. I'm getting fed up writing all this. What's on the next page?

MY OWN STORY

Use this space to write your story

THE STORY OF TRACY BEAKER

Once upon a time there was a little girl called Tracy Beaker. That sounds a bit stupid, like the start of a soppy fairy story. I can't stand fairy stories. They're all the same. If you're very good and very beautiful with long golden curls then, after sweeping up a few cinders or having a long kip in a cobwebby palace, this prince comes along and you live happily ever after. Which is fine if you happen to be a goodie-goodie and look gorgeous. But if you're bad and ugly then you've got no chance whatsoever. You get given a silly name like *Rumpelstiltskin* and nobody invites you to their party and no-one's ever grateful even when you do them a whopping great favour. So of course you get a bit cheesed off with this sort of treatment. You stamp your feet in a rage and fall right through the floorboards or you scream yourself into a frenzy and you get locked up in a tower and they throw away the key.

I've done a bit of stamping and screaming in my time.

And I've been locked up heaps of times. Once they locked me up all day long. And all night. That was at the first Home, when I wouldn't settle because I wanted my mum so much. I was just little then but they still locked me up. I'm not fibbing. Although I do have a tendency to tell a few fibs now and again. It's funny, Aunty Peggy used to call it Telling Fairy Stories.

I'd say something like — 'Guess what, Aunty Peggy, I just met my mum in the back garden and she gave me a ride in her flash new sports car and we went down the shopping arcade and she bought me my very own huge bottle of scent, that posh *Poison* one, just like the bottle Uncle Sid gave you for your birthday, and I was messing about

25

with it, playing Murderers, and the bottle sort of tipped and it's gone all over me as I expect you've noticed, but it's my scent not yours. I don't know what's happened to yours. I think one of the other kids took it.'

You know the sort of thing. I'd make it dead convincing but Aunty Peggy wouldn't even listen properly. She'd just shake her head at me and get all cross and red and say, 'Oh Tracy, you naughty girl, you're Telling Fairy Stories again.' Then she'd give me a smack.

Foster mothers aren't supposed to smack you at all. I told Elaine that Aunty Peggy used to smack me and Elaine sighed and said, 'Well sometimes, Tracy, you really do ask for it.' Which is a lie in itself. I have never in my life said 'Aunty Peggy, please will you give me a great big smack.' And her smacks really hurt too, right on the back of your leg where it stings most. I didn't like that Aunty Peggy at all. If I was in a real fairy story I'd put a curse on her. A huge wart right on the end of her nose? Frogs and toads coming wriggling out of  her mouth every time she tries to speak? No, I can make up better than that. She can have permanent huge great bogeys hanging out of her nose that won't go away no matter how many times she blows it, and whenever she tries to speak she'll make this terribly loud Rude Noise. Great!

26

Oh dear. You can't win. Elaine, my stupid old social worker, was sitting beside me when I started writing THE STORY OF TRACY BEAKER and I got the giggles making up my brilliant curses for Aunty Peggy and Elaine looked surprised and said, 'What are you laughing at, Tracy?'

I said, 'Mind your own business' and she said, 'Now Tracy' and then she looked at what I'd written which is a bit of a cheek seeing as it's supposed to be very private. She sighed when she got to the Aunty Peggy part and said, 'Really Tracy!' and I said, 'Yes, really, Elaine.' And she sighed again and her lips moved for a moment or two. That's her taking a deep breath and counting up to ten. Social workers are supposed to do that when a child is being difficult. Elaine ends up doing an awful lot of counting when she's with me.

When she got to ten she gave me this big false smile. Like this.

'Now look, Tracy,' said Elaine. 'This is your own special book about you, something that you're going to keep for ever. You don't want to spoil it by writing all sorts of silly cheeky rude things in it, do you?'

I said, 'It's my life and it hasn't been very special so far, has it, so why shouldn't I write any old rubbish?'

Then she sighed again, but sympathetically this time, and she put her arm round me and said, 'Hey, I know you've had a hard time, but *you're* very special. You know that, don't you?'

I shook my head and tried to wriggle away.

'Yes, you are, Tracy. Very very special,' Elaine said, hanging on to me.

'Then if I'm so very very special how come no-one wants me?' I said.

'Oh dear, I know it must have been very disappointing for you when your second placement went wrong, love, but you mustn't let it depress you too much. Sooner or later you'll find the perfect placement.'

'A fantastic rich family?'

'Maybe a family. Or maybe a single person, if someone really suitable came along.'

I gave her this long look. 'You're single, Elaine. And I bet you're suitable. So why don't you foster me, eh?'

It was her turn to wriggle then.

'Well, Tracy. You know how it is. I mean, I've got my job. I have to deal with lots of children.'

'But if you fostered me you could stop bothering with all the others and just look after me. They give you money if you foster. I bet they'd give you lots extra because I'm difficult, and I've got behaviour problems and all that. How about it, Elaine? It would be fun, honest it would.'

'I'm sure it would be lots of fun, Tracy, but I'm sorry, it's just not on,' Elaine said.

She tried to give me a big hug but I pushed her hard.

'I was only joking,' I said. 'Yuck. I couldn't stand the thought of living with you. You're stupid and boring and you're all fat and wobbly, I'd absolutely hate the idea of you being my foster mum.'

'I can understand why you're angry with me, Tracy,' said Elaine, trying to look cool and calm, but sucking in her stomach all the same.

I told her I wasn't a bit angry, though I shouted as I said it. I told her I didn't care a bit, though I had these silly watery eyes. I didn't cry though. I don't *ever* cry. Sometimes people think I do, but it's my hay fever.

'I expect you're going to think up all sorts of revolting curses for me now,' said Elaine.

'I'm doing it right this minute,' I told her.
'OK,' she said.

'You always say OK,' I told her. 'You know: OK, that's fine with me, if that's what you want I'm not going to make a fuss; OK Tracy, yes I know you've got this socking great axe in your hand and you're about to chop off my head because you're feeling angry with me, but OK, if that's the way you feel, I'm not going to get worried about it because I'm this super-cool social worker.'

She burst out laughing then.

'No-one can stay super-cool when you're around, Tracy,' she said. 'Look kiddo, you write whatever you want in your life story. It's your own book, after all.'

So that's that. This is my own book and I can write whatever I want. Only I'm not quite sure what I do want, actually. Maybe Elaine *could* help after all. She's over the other side of the sitting-room, helping that wet Peter with his book. He hasn't got a clue. He's filling it all in *so* slowly and *so* seriously, not writing it but printing it with that silly blotchy biro of his, trying to do it ever so carefully but failing miserably, and now he's smudged some of it so it looks a mess anyway.

I've just called Elaine but she says she's got to help Peter for a bit. The poor little petal is getting all worried in case he puts the wrong answers, as if it's some dopey intelligence test. I've done heaps of them, intelligence tests. They're all ever so easy-peasy. I can do them quick as a wink. They always expect kids in care to be as thick as bricks, but I get a hundred out of a hundred nearly every time. Well, they don't tell you the answers, but I bet I do.

TRACY BEAKER IS A STUPID SHOW-OFF AND THIS IS THE SILLIEST LOAD OF RUBBISH I'VE EVER READ AND IF SHE'S SO SUPER-INTELLIGENT HOW COME SHE WETS HER BED LIKE A BABY?

Ignore the stupid scribble up above. It's all lies anyway. It's typical. You can't leave anything for two minutes in this rotten place without one of the other kids spoiling it. But I never thought anyone would stoop so low as to write in my own private life story. And I know who did it too. I know, Justine Littlewood, and you just wait. I'm going to get you.

I went over to rescue Elaine from that boring wimpy little Peter and I had a little peer into his book and I nearly fell over, because you'll never guess who he's put as his best friend. Me. *Me!*

'Is this some sort of joke?' I demanded. He went all red and mumbly and tried to hide what he'd put, but I'd already seen it. *My best friend is Tracy Beaker.* It was down there on the page in black and white. Well, not your actual black and white, more your smudgy blue biro, but you know what I mean.

'Go away and stop pestering poor Peter,' Elaine said to me.

'Yes, but he's putting absolute rubbish in his book, Elaine, and it's stupid. I'm not Peter Ingham's best friend!'

'Well, I think it's very nice that Peter wants you to be his friend,' said Elaine. She pulled a funny face. 'There's no accounting for taste.'

'Oh, ha-ha. Why did you put that, Peter?'

Peter did a little squeak about sharing birthdays and so that made us friends.

'It does *not* make us friends, dumbo,' I declared.

Elaine started getting on at me then, saying I was being nasty to poor little Peetie-Weetie and if I couldn't be friendly why didn't I just push off and get on with my own life story? Well, when people tell me to push off I generally try to stick to them like glue, just to be annoying, so that's what I did.

And then Jenny called me into the kitchen because she made out she wanted a hand getting the lunch ready, but that was just a *ploy*. Jenny doesn't smack. She doesn't even often tell you off. She just uses ploys and tries to distract you. It sometimes works with the thicker kids but it usually has no effect whatsoever on me. However, I quite like helping in the kitchen because you can generally nick a spoonful of jam or a handful of raisins when Jenny's back is turned. So I went along to the kitchen and helped her put an entire shoal of fish fingers under the double grill while she got the chip pan bubbling. Fish fingers don't taste so great when they're raw. I tried nibbling just to see. I don't know why they're called fish *fingers*. They don't have fingers, do they? They ought to be fish *fins*. That Aunty

33

Peggy used to make this awful milk pudding called tapioca which had these little slimy bubbly bits and I told the other kids that they were fish eyes. And I told the really little ones that marmalade is made out of goldfish and they believed that too.

When Jenny started serving out the fish fingers and chips, I went back into the sitting-room to tell everyone that lunch was ready. And I remember seeing Louise and Justine hunched up in a corner, giggling over something they'd got hidden. I don't know. I *am* highly intelligent, I truly wasn't making that up, and yet it was a bit thick of me not to twig what they were up to. Which was reading my own life story and then scribbling all over it.

A little twit like Peter Ingham would tell, but I'm no tell-tale tit. I shall simply get my own back. I shall think long and carefully for a suitable horrible revenge. I don't half hate that Justine. Before she came Louise and I were best friends and we did everything together and, even though I was still dumped in a rotten children's home, it really wasn't so bad. Louise and I made out we were sisters and we had all these secrets and—

One of these secrets was about a certain small problem that I have. A night-time problem. I've got my own room and so it was always a private problem that only Jenny

34

and I knew about. Only to show Louise we were the bestest friends ever I told her about it. I knew it wasn't a sensible move right from the start because she giggled, and she used to tease me about it a bit even when we were still friends. And then she went off with Justine and I'd sometimes worry that she might tell on me, but I always convinced myself she'd never ever stoop that low. Not Louise.

But she has told. She's told Justine, my worst enemy. So what am I going to do to her? Any ideas ticking away inside my head?

Well, I could beat her up.

Tick, tick, tick.
I could deliver a karate chop death blow.

Tick, tick, tick.
I could get my mum to come in her car and run her over, squashing her hedgehog-flat.

Tick, tick, tick. Hey! Tick tock. Tick tock. *I* know. And I also know I'm not leaving this book hanging about. From now on I shall carry it on my person. So, ha-ha, sucks boo to you, Justine Littlewood. Oh you're going to get it. Yes you are, yes you are, tee-hee.

I'm writing this at midnight. I can't put the light on because Jenny might still be prowling about and I don't want *another* ding-dong with her, thanks very much. I'm making do with a torch, only the battery's going, so there's just this dim little glow and I can hardly see what I'm doing. I wish I had something to eat. In all those Enid Blyton school stories they always have midnight feasts. The food sounds a bit weird, sardines and condensed milk, but I could murder a Mars Bar right this minute. Imagine a Mars Bar as big as this bed. Imagine licking it, gnawing away at a corner, scooping out the soft part with both fists. Imagine the wonderful chocolatey smell. I'm slavering at the thought. Yes, that's what those little marks are on the page. Slavers. I don't cry. I don't *ever* cry.

I acted as if I didn't care less when Jenny had a real go at me. And I don't.

'I think you really do care, Tracy,' she said, in that silly sorrowful voice. 'Deep down I think you're really very sorry.'

37

'That's just where you're wrong,' I insisted.

'Come off it now. You must know how you'd feel if your mother had bought you a special present and one of the other kids spoilt it.'

As she said that I couldn't help remembering being in the first Home, long before the dreaded Aunty Peggy or that mean hateful unfair Julie and Ted. My mum came to see me and she'd brought this doll, a doll almost as big as me, with long golden curls and a bright blue lacy dress to match her big blue eyes. I'd never liked dolls all that much but I thought this one was wonderful. I called her Bluebell and I undressed her right down to her frilly white knickers and dressed her up again and brushed her blonde curls and made her blink her big blue eyes, and at night she'd lie in my bed and we'd have these cosy little chats and she'd tell me that Mum was coming back really soon, probably tomorrow, and—

OK, that sort of thing makes me want to puke now but I was only little then and I didn't know any better. The housemother let me cart Bluebell all over the place but she tried to make me give the other kids a go at playing with her. Well, I wasn't going to let that lot maul her about, so of course I didn't let them hold her. But I came unstuck when I started school. You weren't allowed to take toys to school, only on Friday afternoons. I cried and fought but they wouldn't let me. So I had to start leaving Bluebell at home. I'd tuck her up in my bed with her eyes closed, pretending she was asleep, and then when I got home from school I'd charge upstairs into our crummy little dormitory and wake her up with a big hug. Only one day I woke her up and I got the shock of my life. Her eyelids snapped open but her blue eyes had vanished inside her head. Some rotten lousy pig had given them a good poke. I couldn't stand it, seeing those creepy empty sockets. She stopped being my friend. She just scared me.

The housemother took Bluebell off to this dolls' hospital and they gave her some new eyes. They were blue too, but not the same bright blue, and they didn't blink properly either. They either got stuck altogether or they flashed up and down all the time, making her look silly and fluttery. But I didn't really care then. She was spoilt. She wasn't the same Bluebell. She didn't talk to me any more.

I never found out which kid had done it. The housemother said it was A Mystery. Just One Of Those Things.

Jenny didn't call it a mystery when Justine went sobbing to her because her silly old Mickey Mouse alarm clock had got broken.

39

Clocks break all the time. It's not as if it's a really flash expensive clock. If I'd been Jenny I'd have told Justine to stop making such a silly fuss. I'd have stopped up my ears when that sneaky little twerp started going on about me. 'I bet I know who did it too, Jenny. *That Tracy Beaker*.'

Yes, she sneaked on me. And Jenny listened, because she came looking for me. She had to look quite a long time. I kind of suspected what was coming, so I cleared off. I didn't try to hide in the house or the garden like one of the little kids. I'm not that dumb. They can flush you out in five minutes no matter where you are. No, I skipped it out the back door and down the road and went for a wander round the town.

It was great. Yes, I had the most amazing time. First I went to McDonald's and had a Big Mac and french fries with a strawberry milk shake and then I went to the pictures

40

and saw this really funny film and I laughed
so much I fell out of my seat and then I went
off with this whole crowd of friends to an
amusement arcade and I kept winning the
jackpot on the fruit machines and then we
all went off to this party and I drank a whole
bottle of wine and it was great, it just tasted
like lemonade, and this girl there, we made
friends and she asked me if I'd like to stay the
night, sharing her twin beds in this fantastic
pink and white room, in fact she said I could
stay there permanently if I really wanted and
so I said . . .

I said: 'No thanks, I'd sooner go back to
my crummy children's home.' ?

Of course I didn't say that. Well, she didn't say it either. I sort of made her up. And her party. I didn't go down the amusement arcade. Or to the pictures. Or McDonald's. I *would* have done, but I couldn't, on account of the fact I ran off with no cash whatsoever.

I said I tell fibs sometimes. It makes things more interesting. I mean, what's the point of writing what I really did? Which was loaf about the town feeling more and more fed up. The only thing I could think of to do was sit in the bus shelter. It got a bit boring. I pretended I was waiting for a bus and I tried to think of all the places I'd like to go to. But that began to depress me because I started thinking about Watford, where my mum said she lived. And last year I got all the right money together (which created a few problems afterwards as I sort of borrowed it without asking) and sussed out the journey and got all these trains and buses and all the rest of it, so that I could pay my mum a visit and give her a lovely surprise. Only it was me that got the surprise because she wasn't there, and the people who lived in that house said she'd moved on about six months ago and they didn't have a clue where she'd gone now.

So it's going to take a bit of organized searching to find her again. I could catch a different bus every day for the rest of my life and maybe not find her. It's hard when you haven't got a clue where to look.

I was still scrunched up in the bus shelter when a familiar white Minivan hoved into view. It was Mike, come looking for me. Mike looks after us with Jenny. He isn't half a bore. He doesn't often get cross but he whinges on about Rules and Responsibility and a whole lot of other rubbish.

So by the time I'd got back to the Home I was sick to death of the subject, but then Jenny came into my bedroom and *she* started. And she assumed it was me that broke Justine's clock though she had no proof whatsoever. I told her so, and said she just

liked picking on me, and it wasn't fair. She said I'd feel better if I owned up to breaking Justine's clock and then went to say sorry to her. I said she had to be joking. I wasn't the slightest bit sorry and anyway I didn't didn't *didn't* break Justine's rotten clock.

That isn't necessarily a fib. I don't absolutely one hundred percent *know* that I broke it. All right, I did go into her bedroom when she was in the bathroom, and I did pick up the clock to look at it. Well, she's always going on about it because she's got this boring thing about her dad. She makes out he's so flipping special when he hardly ever comes to see her. The only thing he's ever given her is that stupid tinny old alarm clock. I wanted to look at it to see if it was really so special. Well, it wasn't. I bet he just got it from Woolworth's. And it certainly wasn't made very carefully because when I twiddled the knobs to make the little Mickey on the end of the hands go whizzing round and round he couldn't keep it up for very long. There was this sudden whir and clunk and then the hand fell off altogether and Mickey fell too, with his little paws in the air, dead.

But he might have been about to take his last gasp anyway. That hand might well have fallen off the next time Justine touched the stupid clock to wind it up.

I'm not going to say sorry no matter what.
I wish I could get to sleep.
I'll try counting sheep . . .

I *still* can't get to sleep and it's the middle
of the night now and it's rotten and I keep
thinking about my mum. I wish she'd come
and get me. I wish anyone would come and
get me. Why can't I ever get a good foster
family? That Aunty Peggy and Uncle Sid were
lousy. But then I could suss them out and tell
they were lousy right from the start. Anyone
who smacks hard and serves up frogspawn for
your pudding is certainly not an ideal aunty.
But last time, when I got fostered by Julie
and Ted, I really thought it was all going to
work out happily ever after, and that it was
my turn to be the golden princess instead of
a *Rumpelstiltskin*.

They were great at first, Julie and Ted. That's what I called them right from the start. They didn't want to be a prissy aunty and uncle. And Julie said she didn't want me to call her Mum because I already had a mum. I thought such a lot of Julie when she said that. She wasn't exactly my idea of a glamorous foster mum – she had this long wispy brown hair and she wore sludge-coloured smocky things and sandals – and Ted looked a bit of a wimp too with his glasses and his beard and weirdo comfy walking shoes, not so much

Hush Puppy as Shut-your-face Hound-Dog –
but I thought they were the sort of couple you
could really trust. Ha!

Because I went to live with them and
I thought we were getting on really great,
though they were a bit boringly strict about
stuff like sweets and bedtimes and horror
videos, but then Julie started to wear bigger
smocks than ever and lolled about on the sofa
and Ted got all misty-eyed behind his glasses
and I started to realize that something was
up. And so I asked them what it was and
they hedged and pulled faces at each other
and then they looked shifty and told me that
everything was fine and I knew they were
lying. Things weren't fine at all.

They didn't even have the guts to tell me
themselves. They left it to Elaine. She'd only
just started to be my social worker then (I've
had heaps because they kept moving around
and leaving me behind and I got passed on
like a parcel). I wasn't that keen on Elaine
in those days. In fact I was really narked
with her, because I'd had this man social
worker Terry before her and he used to call
me Smartie and he used to give me the odd
tube of Smarties too, and I felt Elaine was a
very poor substitute.

I wish I hadn't thought of those Smarties.
I wish I had some now, I'm simply starving.

I'm sure Elaine marked me down as Sulky and Non-co-operative in her little notebook. The day she told me the Julie and Ted Bombshell I'm sure she scribbled TRACY TOTALLY GOB-SMACKED. Because Julie was having her own baby, after years of thinking she couldn't have any kids.

I didn't get it at first.

'So what's the problem, Elaine?' I said. 'We'll be a proper family then, four of us instead of three.'

Elaine was having difficulties finding the right words. She kept opening her mouth and closing it again, not saying a sausage.

'You look just like a fish when you do that, did you know?' I said cheekily, because my heart was starting to hammer hard against my chest and I knew that when Elaine eventually got the words out I wouldn't like the sound of them.

'The thing is, Tracy . . . Well, Julie and Ted have loved fostering you, and they've got very fond of you, but . . . you see, now they're having their own baby they feel that they're not really going to be able to cope.'

'Oh, I get it,' I said, in this jokey silly voice. 'So they're going to give the boring old baby away because they can't cope with it. And keep me. Because they had me first, didn't they?'

'Tracy—'

'They're not really going to dump me, are they?'

'They still very much want to keep in touch with you and—'

'So why can't I go on living with them? Look, I'll help all I can. Julie doesn't need to worry. I'll be just like a second mum to this baby. I know all what to do. I can give it its bottle and change its soggy old nappy and thump it on its back to bring up its wind. I'm dead experienced where babies are concerned.'

'Yes, I know, Tracy. But that's the trouble. You see, when Julie and Ted first fostered you, we did tell them a bit about your background, and the trouble you had in your first foster home. You know, when you shut the baby up in the cupboard—'

'That was Steve. And he wasn't a baby. He was a foul little toddler, and he kept mucking up our bedroom so I tidied him up into the cupboard just for a bit so I could get everything straightened out.'

'And there was the ghost game that got totally out of hand—'

'Oh that! All those little kids *loved* that game. I was ever so good at finding the right hiding places and then I'd start an eerie sort of moan and then I'd jump out at them, wearing this old white sheet.'

49

'And everyone got scared silly.'

'No they didn't. They just squealed because they were excited. *I* was the one who should have been scared, because they were all the ghost-busters you see, and I was the poor little ghost and—'

'OK, OK, but the point is, Tracy, it makes it plain in your records that you don't always get on well with little children.'

'That's a whopping great lie! What about Camilla? I looked after her at that children's home and she loved me, she really did.'

'Yes, I'm sure that's true, Tracy, but— Well, the thing is, Julie and Ted still feel they don't want to take any chances. They're worried you might feel a bit uncomfortable with a baby in the house.'

'So they're pushing me out?'

'But like I said, they still want to keep in touch with you and maybe take you out for tea sometimes.'

'No way,' I said. 'I don't want to see them ever again.'

'Oh Tracy, that's silly. That's just cutting off your own nose to spite your face,' said Elaine.

That's such a daft expression. How on earth would you go about it?

It wouldn't half hurt.

It hurt a lot leaving Julie and Ted's.

50

They wanted me to stay for a few months but I couldn't clear out of there quick enough. So here I am in this dump. They've tried to see me twice but I wasn't having any of it. I don't want any visitors, thanks very much. Apart from my mum. I wonder where she is. And why didn't she leave a forwarding address at that last place? And how will she ever get to find me here? Yeah, that's the problem. I bet she's been trying and trying to get hold of me, but she doesn't know where to look. Last time I saw her I was at Aunty Peggy's. I bet Mum's been round to Aunty Peggy's and I bet that silly old smacking-machine wouldn't tell her where I'd gone. So I bet my mum got really mad with her. And if she found out just how many times that Aunty Peggy smacked me then wow, ker-pow, splat, bang, I bet my mum would really let her have it.

I don't half want my mum.

I know why I can't sleep. It's because I'm so starving hungry, that's why. Crying always makes me hungry. Not that I've been crying now. I don't *ever* cry.

I think maybe I'll try slipping down to the kitchen. Jenny's bound to be fast asleep by now. Yeah, that's what I'll do.

I'm back. I've had my very own midnight feast. And it was absolutely delicious too. Well, it wasn't bad. I couldn't find any chocolate, of course, and that was what I really fancied. But I found an opened packet of cornflakes and got stuck into them, and then I tried raiding the fridge. There weren't too many goodies. I didn't go a bundle on tomorrow's uncooked mince or yesterday's cold custard, but I poked my finger in the butter and then dabbled it in the sugar bowl and that tasted fine. I did quite a lot of poking and dabbling actually. I know Jenny might notice so I got my little finger nail and drew these weeny lines like teethmarks and then did some paw prints all over the butter, so she'd think it was a mouse. Mice do eat butter, don't they? They like cheese, which is the same sort of thing. Of course this is going to have to be a mountaineering mouse, armed with ice-pick and climbing boots, able to trek

up the grim north face of the Frigidaire. And then it's got to develop Mighty Mouse muscles to prise open the door of the fridge to get at the feast inside.

Maybe Jenny will still be a teensy bit suspicious. But I can't help that. At least she didn't catch me while I was noshing away at my midnight feast.

Someone else did though. Not in the kitchen. Afterwards, when I was sneaking up the stairs again. They're very dark, these stairs, and they take a bit of careful negotiating. One of the little kids is quite likely to leave a teddy or a rattle or a building brick halfway up and you can come an awful cropper and wake the entire household. So I was feeling my way very very cautiously when I heard this weird little moaning sound coming from up on the landing. So I looked up, sharpish, and I could just make out this pale little figure, all white and trailing, and it was so exactly like a ghost that I opened my mouth to scream.

But Tracy Beaker has a lot of bottle. I'm not scared of anybody. Not even ghosts. So I clapped my hand over my mouth to stop the scream and pattered right on up the stairs to confront this puny little piece of ectoplasm. Only it wasn't a ghost after all. It was just snivelling drivelling Peter Ingham, clutching some sheets.

'Whatever are you up to, creep?' I whispered.

'Nothing,' Peter whispered back.

'Oh sure. You just thought you'd take your sheets for a walk in the middle of the night,' I said.

Peter flinched away from me.

'You've wet them, haven't you?' I said.

'No,' Peter mumbled. He's a useless liar.

'Of course you've wet them. And you've been trying to wash them out in the bathroom, I know. So that people won't guess.'

'Oh don't tell, Tracy, please,' Peter begged.

'What do you take me for? I'm no tell-tale,' I said. 'And look, you don't have to fuss. Just get Jenny on her own in the morning and whisper to her. She'll sort it all out for you. She doesn't get cross.'

'Really?'

'Truly. And what you do now, you get yourself some dry sheets from the airing cupboard, right? And some pyjamas. Goodness, you don't know anything, do you? How long have you been in care?'

'Three months, one week, two days,' said Peter.

'Is that all? I've been in and out of care nearly all my life,' I said, getting the sheets for him. 'So why are you here now then? Your mum and dad get fed up with you? Can't say as I blame them.'

'They died when I was little. So I lived with my nan. But then she got old and then– then she died too,' Peter mumbled. 'And I didn't have anyone else so I had to come here. And I don't like it.'

'Well, of course you don't like it. But this is a lot better than most children's homes. You ought to have tried some of the places I've been in. They lock you up and they beat you and they practically starve you to death and then when they do give you meals it's absolutely disgusting, they pretend it's meat but it's really chopped up worms and dried dog's muck and—'

'Shut up, Tracy,' Peter said, holding his stomach.

'Who are you telling to shut up?' I said, but not really fiercely. 'Go on, you'd better shove off back to your room. And put your dry pyjamas on. You're shivering.'

'OK, Tracy. Thanks.' He paused, fidgeting and fumbling with his sheets. 'I wish you would be my friend, Tracy.'

'I don't really bother making friends,' I said. 'There's not much point, because my mum's probably coming to get me soon and then I'll be living with her so I won't need any friends here.'

'Oh,' said Peter, and he sounded really disappointed.

'Still. I suppose you can be my friend just for now,' I said.

I don't know why I said it. Who wants to be lumbered with a silly little creep like that? I'm too kind-hearted, that's my trouble.

There wasn't much point in getting to sleep, because when I did eventually nod off I just had these stupid nightmares. It's as if there's a video inside my head and it switches itself on the minute my eyes close and I keep hoping it's going to be showing this great comedy that'll have me in stitches but then the creepy music starts and I know I'm in for it. Last night was the Great Horror Movie of all time. I was stuck in the dark somewhere and there was something really scary coming up quick behind me so I had to run like mad. Then I got to this big round pool and there were these stepping stones with people perching on them and I jumped on to the first one and there was no room at all because that fat Aunty Peggy was spread all over it. I tried to cling to her but she gave me a big smack and sent me flying. So then I jumped on to the next stepping stone and Julie and Ted were there and I tried to grab hold of them but they just turned their backs on me and didn't even try to catch me when I fell and so I had to try to reach the next stepping stone but I was in the water doing my doggy-paddle

and it was getting harder and harder, and every time I swam to a stepping stone all these people prodded at me with sticks and pushed me away and I kept going under the water and . . .

. . . and then I woke up and I know that whenever I dream about water it spells Trouble with a capital T. I had to make my own dash to the airing cupboard and the laundry basket. I was unfortunate enough to bump into Justine too. She didn't look as if she'd slept much either. Her eyes seemed a bit on the red side. I couldn't help feeling a bit mean then, in spite of everything. So I gave her this big smile and I said, 'I'm sorry about what happened to your alarm clock, Justine.'

I didn't exactly tell her that *I* did it. Because I still don't know that it really was me. And anyway, I'd be a fool to admit it, wouldn't I? But I told her that I was still sorry, just like Jenny had suggested.

Only there's no point trying to be nice to pigs like Justine Littlewood. She didn't smile back and graciously accept my apologies.

'You'll be even sorrier when I've finished with you, Tracy Beaker,' she hissed. 'And what have you been doing, eh? Wet the bed again? Baby!' She hissed a lot more too. Stupid insulting things. I'm not going to waste my time writing them all down. Words can't hurt me anyway. Only I can't help being just a bit worried about that threat. What's she going to do to get her own back for the clock? If only we had poxy locks on our bedroom doors. Still, at least we've got separate bedrooms in this Home, even though they're weeny like cupboards.

It's new policy. Children in care need their own space. And I want to stay in my own space, doing all this writing, but Jenny has just put her head round my door and told me to buzz out into the garden with the others. And I said No Fear. Being in a Home is lousy at the best of times, but I just can't stick it in the school holidays when you're all cooped up together and the big ones bully you and the little ones pester you and the ones your own age gang up on you and have secrets together and call you names.

'How's about trying to make it up with Justine?' Jenny suggested, coming to sit on my bed.

So I snorted and told her she was wasting her time, and more to the point, she was wasting *my* time, because I wanted to get on with my writing.

'You've done ever such a lot, Tracy,' said Jenny, looking at all these pages. 'We'll be running out of paper soon.'

'Then I'll use the backs of birthday cards. Or bog roll. Anything. I'm inspired, see. I can't stop.'

'Yes, you've really taken to this writing. Going to be a writer when you grow up, eh?'

'Maybe.' I hadn't thought about it before. I was always sure I was going to be on telly with my own chat show. THE TRACY BEAKER EXPERIENCE and I'd walk out on to this stage in a sparkly dress and all the studio audience would clap and cheer and all these really famous celebrities would fight tooth and nail to get on my show to speak to me. But I reckon I could write books too.

'Tell you what, Tracy. We've got a real writer coming round some time this afternoon. You could ask her for a few tips.'

'What's she coming for?'

'Oh, she's doing this article for a magazine about children in care.'

'Oh that boring old stuff,' I said, pretending to yawn but inside I start fizzing away.

I wouldn't mind my story being written up in some magazine. A book would be better of course, but maybe that could come later. I'd have to be careful what she said about me though. Elaine the Pain made a right mess of my newspaper advert. I was Child of the Week in the local paper. If she'd only let me write it I'd have been bowled over by people rushing to adopt dear little Tracy Beaker. I know just how to present myself in the right sort of way.

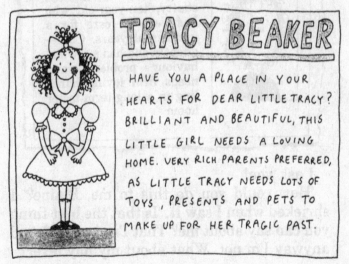

TRACY BEAKER

HAVE YOU A PLACE IN YOUR HEARTS FOR DEAR LITTLE TRACY? BRILLIANT AND BEAUTIFUL, THIS LITTLE GIRL NEEDS A LOVING HOME. VERY RICH PARENTS PREFERRED, AS LITTLE TRACY NEEDS LOTS OF TOYS, PRESENTS AND PETS TO MAKE UP FOR HER TRAGIC PAST.

Elaine is useless. Doesn't have a clue. She didn't even let me get specially kitted out for the photograph.

'We want you looking natural, Tracy,' she said.

Well I turned out looking too flipping natural. Hair all over the place and a scowl on my face because that stupid photographer kept treating me like a baby, telling me to Watch the Birdie. And the things Elaine wrote about me!

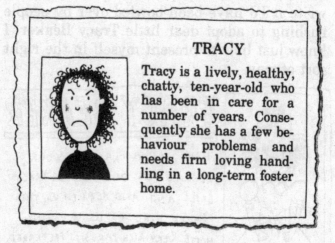

TRACY

Tracy is a lively, healthy, chatty, ten-year-old who has been in care for a number of years. Consequently she has a few behaviour problems and needs firm loving handling in a long-term foster home.

I ask you!

'How could you *do* this to me, Elaine?' I shrieked when I saw it. 'Is that the best thing you can say about me? That I'm *healthy*? And anyway I'm not. What about my hay fever?'

'I also say you're lively. And chatty.'

'Yeah. Well, we all know what that means. Cheeky. Difficult. Bossy.'

'You said it, Tracy,' Elaine murmured.

'And all this guff about behaviour problems! What do I do, eh? I don't go round beating people up? Well, not many. And I don't smash the furniture. Hardly ever.'

'Tracy, it's very understandable that you have a few problems—'

'I *don't*! And then how could you ask for someone to handle me *firmly*?'

'And lovingly,' said Elaine. 'I put loving too.'

'Oh yes, they'll tell me how much they love me as they lay into me with a cane. Honestly, Elaine, you're round the twist. You're just going to attract a bunch of creepy child-beaters with this crummy advert.'

But it didn't even attract them. No-one replied at all.

Elaine kept telling me not to worry, as if it was somehow my fault. I know if she'd only get her act together and do a really flash advert there'd be heaps of offers. I bet.

But maybe I'm wasting my time nagging Elaine. This woman who's coming this afternoon might be just the chance I've been waiting for. If she's a real writer then she'll know how to jazz it all up so that I sound really fantastic. Only I've got to present myself to

63

her in a special way so that she'll pick me out from all the others and just do a feature on me. So what am I going to do, eh?

Aha!

Not aha. More like boo-hoo. Only I don't ever cry, of course.

I don't want to write down what happened. I don't think I want to be a writer any more.

I tried, I really did. I went flying up to my bedroom straight after lunch and I did my best to make myself look pretty. I know my hair is untidy so I tried scragging it back into these little sticky-out plaits. Camilla had little plaits and everyone cooed over them and said how cute she looked. I thought my face looked a bit bare when I'd done the plaits so I wetted some of the side bits with spit and tried to make them go into curls.

I still looked a bit boring so I decided to liven my face up a bit. So I sneaked round to Adele's room. She's sixteen and she's got a Saturday job in BHS and she's got a drawer absolutely chock-a-block with make-up. I borrowed a bit of blusher to give myself some colour in my cheeks. And then I thought I'd try out a pink glossy lipstick too. And mascara to make my eyelashes look long. I tried a bit on my eyebrows too, to make them stand out. And I put a lot of powder on to be

like the icing on a cake. I thought I looked OK when I'd finished. Well, at least I looked different.

I changed my clothes too. I didn't want this writer to see me in a scrubby old T-shirt and skirt. No way. It had to be posh frock time. Only I don't really have a posh frock of my own. I did try on a few of Adele's things but somehow they didn't really suit me.

So then I started thinking about all the other girls. Louise had this really fantastic frock that she got a couple of years ago from some auntie. A real posh party frock with smocking and a flouncy skirt and its own sewn-in frilly white petticoat. It was a bit small for her now, of course, but she could just about squeeze into it for special days. And Louise and I are about the same size.

I knew Louise would go spare if she saw me parading around in her best party frock but I decided it might be worth it if I made a great impression on the writer woman first. So I beetled along the corridor towards her room, but I didn't have any luck. Louise was in her room. With Justine. I heard their voices.

They were discussing me, actually. And nappies. They were snorting with laughter and normally I'd have marched right in and punched their silly smirky faces but I knew if I got into a fight Jenny would send me to my room and make me stay there and I'd miss out on meeting the woman writer.

So with *extreme* self-control I walked away, still musing on what I was going to wear. I know it's summer, but I'd started to feel a bit shaky and shivery so I put on this mohair sweater that Julie knitted me for Christmas. When Julie and Ted dumped me I vowed not to have anything to do with them and I even thought about cutting up the mohair sweater into little woolly hankies but I couldn't quite do it. It's a pretty fantastic sweater actually, with the name Tracy in bright blue letters. That way it's obvious it's mine, specially made for me. Of course it's a bit tickly and prickly, but my mum once said you have to suffer if you want to look beautiful.

She's always looked beautiful. I don't half wish I took after her. I wasn't too bad as a baby. I was still quite cute as a toddler. But then I went off in a big way.

Still, I was trying my hardest to look OK. I only had my old skirt to wear with my mohair sweater, and there were dark blue stains all down one side where a biro exploded in my pocket, but I couldn't help that. The woman writer might just think it was a tie-and-dye effect. And at least the blue matched the lettering on my jumper.

I kept on prinking and preening in my room. I heard all the other kids go clattering downstairs. I heard Louise and Justine go giggle-snigger-titter along the corridor. My face started burning so that I didn't need my blusher. Then I heard Adele rampaging around because some rotten so-and-so had been in her room and rifled through all her make-up and mucked it all up. I decided to hang about in my room a bit longer.

I heard the front door bell. I heard Jenny talking to someone down in the hall. I heard them go into the sitting-room. I knew it was time to make my Entrance.

So I went running down the stairs and barging into the sitting-room with this great big smile on my face. It's no use looking sad or sulky if you want people to like you. Mum always tells me to give her a big smile. Even when she's saying goodbye to me. You can't look gloomy or it just upsets people and they don't want any more to do with you.

You've got to have this great big s-s-s-m-m-m-i-i-i-l-l-l-e-e-e.

Everyone looked up at me when I went into the sitting-room. And they all smiled too. Just for a moment I was daft enough to think they were all smiling back at me. But then I saw they were the wrong sort of smiles. They were smirks. And Justine and Louise nudged each other and giggled and spluttered and whooped. And Adele glared at me. Peter Ingham was the only one with a proper smile. He came over to me. He was blinking a bit rapidly.

'You look . . . nice, Tracy,' he said.

But I knew he was lying. It was no use kidding myself. It was obvious I looked a right prat. Jenny's pretty laid back about appearances but even she looked shocked at the sight of me. And it looked like all that effort was for nothing, because she didn't seem to have the woman writer person with her after all.

I've seen women writers on chat shows on the telly. They're quite glamorous, like film stars, with glittery frocks and high heels and lots of jewellery. They look a bit like my mum, only nowhere near as pretty of course.

The woman with Jenny looked like some boring social worker or teacher. Scruffy brown hair. No make-up. Scrubby T-shirt and rumpled jeans. A bit like me on an off-day, grown up.

I decided to slope off back to my bedroom. It seemed sensible to steer clear of Adele anyway. But Jenny caught hold of me by the back of my jumper.

'Hang about, Tracy. I thought you wanted to meet Cam Lawson.'

'Who?' I said.

'You know. The writer. I told you,' Jenny hissed. Then she lowered her voice even more. 'Why are you wearing your winter jumper when it's boiling hot today? And what on earth have you done to your face?'

'She thinks she looks pretty,' said Justine, and she clutched Louise and they both shrieked.

'Pipe down, you two,' said Jenny. 'Tracy. Tracy!' She hung on to me firmly, stopping me barging over to that stupid pair of titterers so as I could bang their heads together. 'Leave them, Tracy. Come and meet Cam.'

I wanted to meet this Cam (what sort of a silly name is that?) even though she didn't look a bit like a *proper* writer, but I sort of hung back. I'm usually the last person to feel shy, but somehow I suddenly didn't know what to say or what to do. So I growled something at Jenny and twisted away from her and stood in a corner by myself, just watching.

Peter came trotting after me. Justine and Louise were still having hysterics at my appearance. You could tell they'd actually got over the giggles by this time, but Justine kept going into further false whoops and Louise was almost as bad.

'Don't take any notice of them,' Peter whispered.

'I don't,' I said crossly.

'I like your jumper,' said Peter. 'And your make-up. And the new hairstyle.'

'Then you're mad. It looks a mess. I look a mess. I look a mess *on purpose*,' I said fiercely. 'So you needn't feel sorry for me, Peter Ingham. You just clear off and leave me alone, right?'

Peter fidgeted from one foot to the other, looking worried.

'Clear off, you stupid little creep,' I said.

So of course he did clear off then. I wondered why I'd said it. OK, he *is* a creep, but he's not really that bad. I'd said he could be my friend. And it was a lot better when he was with me than standing all by myself, watching everyone over the other side of the room clustered round this Cam person calling herself a writer.

She's a weird sort of woman if you ask me. She was chatting away and yet you could tell she was really nervous inside. She

kept fidgeting with her pen and notebook and I was amazed to see she bites her nails! She's a great big grown-up woman and yet she does a dopey kid's thing like that. Well, she's not great big, she's little and skinny, but even so!

My mum has the most beautiful fingernails, very long and pointy and polished. She varnishes them every day. I just love that smell of nail varnish, that sharp peardrop niff that makes your nostrils twitch. Jenny caught me happily sniffing nail varnish one day, and do you know what she thought? Only that I was inhaling it, like glue sniffing. Did you ever? I let her think it too. *I* wasn't going to tell her I just liked the smell because it reminds me of Mum.

I'll tell you another weird thing about Cam Whatsit. She sat on one of our rickety old chairs, her legs all draped round the rungs, and she talked *to* the children. Most adults that come here talk *at* children.

They tell you what to do.

They go on and on about themselves.

They talk about you.

They ask endless stupid questions.

They make personal comments.

Even the social workers are at it. Or they strike this special nothing-you-can-say-would-shock-me-sweetie pose and they make stupid statements.

'I guess you're feeling really angry and upset today, Tracy,' they twitter, when I've wrecked my bedroom or got into a fight or shouted and sworn at someone, so that it's *obvious* I'm angry and upset.

They do this to show me that they understand. Only they don't understand peanuts. *They're* not the ones in care. I am.

I thought Cam Thing would ask questions and take down case histories in her notebook, all brisk and organized. But from what I could make out over in the corner she had a very different way of doing things.

She smiled a bit and fidgeted a lot and sort of weighed everybody up, and they all had a good stare at her. Two of the little kids

73

tried to climb up on to her lap because they do that to anyone who sits down. It's not because they *like* the person, it's just they like being cuddled. They'd cry to have a cuddle with a cross-eyed gorilla, I'm telling you.

Most strangers to children's homes get all flattered and make a great fuss of the littlies and come on like Mary Poppins. This Cam seemed a bit surprised, even a bit put out. I don't blame her. Little Wayne in particular has got the runniest nose of all time and he likes to bury his head affectionately into your chest, wiping it all down your front.

Cam held him at arm's length, and when he tried his burrowing trick she distracted him by giving him her pen. He liked flicking the catch up and down.

She let little Becky have a ride on her foot at the same time, so she didn't feel left out and bawl. Becky kept trying to climb up her leg, pulling her jean up. Some of Cam's leg got exposed. It was a pretty ropey sort of leg if you ask me. A bit hairy for a start. My mum always shaves her legs, and she wears sheer see-through tights to show them off. This Cam had socks like a schoolgirl. Only they were quite funny brightly patterned socks. I thought the red and yellow bits were just squares at first, but then I got a bit closer and saw they were books. I wouldn't mind having

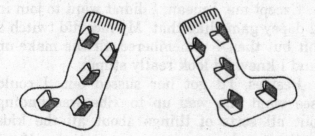

a pair of socks like that myself, if I'm going to write all these books.

She's written books. Old Cammy. Cammy-knicker, ha-ha. The other kids asked her and she told them. She said she wrote some stories but they didn't sell much so she also wrote some romantic stuff. She doesn't look the romantic type to me.

Adele got interested then because she loves all those soppy love books and Cam told her some titles and the boys all tittered and went yuck yuck and Jenny got a bit narked but Cam said she didn't mind, they were mostly yuck but she couldn't help it if that's what people liked to read.

Then they all started talking about reading. Maxy said he liked this book *Where the Wild Things Are* because the boy in that is called Max, and Cam said she knew that book and she made a Wild Thing face and then everyone else did too.

Except me. I mean, I didn't want to join in a dopey game like that. My face did twitch a bit but then I remembered all the make-up and I knew I'd look really stupid.

Besides, I'd got her sussed out. I could see what she was up to. She was finding out all sorts of things about all the kids without asking any nosy questions. Maxy went on about his dad being a Wild Thing. Adele went on about love, only of course real life wasn't like that, and love didn't ever last and people split up and sometimes didn't even go on loving their children.

Even little creepy Peter piped up about these Catherine Cookson books that his nan used to like, and he told Cam how he used to read them to her because her eyes had gone all blurry. And then *his* eyes went a bit blurry too, remembering his nan, and Cam's hand reached out sort of awkwardly. She didn't quite manage to hold his hand, she just sort of tapped his bony wrist sympathetically.

'My nan's dead too. And my mum. They're both together in heaven now. Angels, like,' said Louise, lisping a bit.

She always does that. Puts on this sweet little baby act when there are grown-ups about. Like she was a little angel herself. Ha. Our little Louise can be even worse than me when she wants. She's had three foster placements, no, was it four? Anyway, none of them worked out. But Louise always swore she didn't care. We used to have this pact that we'd do our best not to get fostered at all and we'd stay together at the Home till we got to be eighteen and then we'd get them to house us together. In our own modern flat. We'd got it all planned out. Louise even started thinking about our furniture, the ornaments, the posters on the walls.

And then Justine came and everything was spoilt. Oh how I hate that Justine Littlewood. I'm glad I broke her silly Mickey Mouse alarm clock. I'd like to break her into little bits and all.

Anyway, Louise lisped on about angels and I'll give that Cam her due, she didn't go all simpering and sentimental and pat Louise on her curly head and talk about the little darling. She stayed calm and matter-of-fact, and started talking about angels and wondering what they would look like.

'That's simple, Miss. They've got these big wings and long white nighties and those gold plate things stuck on the back of their heads,' said Justine.

'Draw one for me,' said Cam, offering her pen and notebook.

'OK,' said Justine, though she can't draw for toffee. Then she had a close look at the pen in her hand. 'Here, it's a Mickey Mouse pen. Look, Louise, see the little Mickey. Oh Miss, where did you get this pen? It's great! I love Mickey, I do. I've got this Mickey Mouse alarm clock, my dad gave it me, only some *pig* broke it deliberately.' Justine looked over her shoulder and glared at me.

I glared back, making out I couldn't care less. And I *couldn't*. My face started burning, but that was just because of my mohair sweater.

Justine drew her stupid angel and Cam nodded at it.

'Yes, that's the way people usually draw angels.' She looked at Louise. 'So is this the way you imagine your mum and your nan?'

'Well. Sort of,' said Louise.

'Is that the sort of nightie that your nan would wear? And what about the halo, the gold plate bit. Would that fit neatly on top of her hairstyle?'

Louise giggled uncertainly, not sure what she was getting at.

'You draw me what you think your mum and nan look like as angels,' said Cam.

Louise started, but she can't draw much either, and she kept scribbling over what she'd done.

'This is silly,' she said, giving up.

I knew what Cam was on about. I'd have

done a really great drawing of Louise's mum
and nan in natty angel outfits. Like this.

'I'll draw you an angel, Miss,' said Maxy,
grabbing at the pen. 'I'll draw me as an angel
and I'll have big wings so I can fly like an
aeroplane, y-e-e-e-o-o-o-w, y-e-e-e-o-o-o-w.' He
went on making his dopey aeroplane noises all
the time he was drawing.

Then the others had a go, even the big
ones. I got a bit nearer and craned my neck
to see what they'd all drawn. I didn't think
any of them very inspired.

I knew exactly what I'd draw if she asked
me. It wouldn't be a silly old angel.

Then Cam looked up. She caught my eye. She did ask me.

'Have a go?' she said, dead casual.

I gave this little shrug as if I couldn't care less. Then I sauntered forward, very slowly. I held out my hand for the pen.

'This is Tracy,' said Jenny, poking her big nose in. 'She's the one who wants to be a writer.'

I felt my face start burning again.

'What, her?' said Justine. 'You've got to be joking.'

'Now Justine,' said Jenny. 'Tracy's written heaps and heaps in her Life Book.'

'Yeah, but it's all rubbish,' said Justine, and her hand shot out and she made a grab underneath my jumper, where I was keeping this book for safety. I bashed out at her but I wasn't quick enough. She snatched the book from me before I could stop her.

'Give that here!' I shrieked.

'It's rubbish, I tell you, listen,' said Justine, and she opened my book and started reading in a silly high-pitched baby voice "Once upon a time there was a little girl called Tracy Beaker and that sounds stupid and no wonder because I *am* stupid and I wet the bed and— Ooooowwww!" '

Things got a bit hazy after that. But I got my book back. And Justine's nose became a wonderful scarlet fountain. I was glad glad glad. I wanted her whole body to spout blood but Jenny had hold of me by this time and she was shouting for Mike and I got hauled off to the Quiet Room. Only I wasn't quiet in there. I yelled my head off. I went on yelling when Jenny came to try and calm me down. And then Jenny went away and someone else came into the room. I wasn't sure who it was at first because when I yell my eyes screw up and I can't see properly. Then I made out the jeans and the T-shirt and the shock of hair and I knew it was Cam Whosit and that made me burn all over until I felt like a junior Joan of Arc.

There was me, throwing a hairy fit, and there was her standing there watching me. I don't care about people like Jenny or Elaine seeing me. They're used to it. Nearly all children in care have a roaring session once in a while. I have them more than once, actually. And I usually just let rip, but now I felt like a right raving loony in front of her.

But I didn't stop yelling all the same. There was no point. She'd already seen me at it. And heard me too. She didn't try to stop me. She wasn't saying a word. She was standing there. And she had this awful expression on her face. I couldn't stand it. She looked sorry for me.

I wasn't having that. So I told her to go away. That's putting it politely. I yelled some very rude words at her. And she just sort of shrugged and nodded and went off.

I was left screaming and swearing away, all by myself.

But I'm OK now. I'm not in the Quiet Room any more. I stayed in there ever such a long time and I even had my tea in there on a tray but now I'm in my bedroom and I've been writing and writing and writing away and it looks like I can't *help* being a writer. I've written so much I've got a big lump on the longest finger of my right hand. You look.

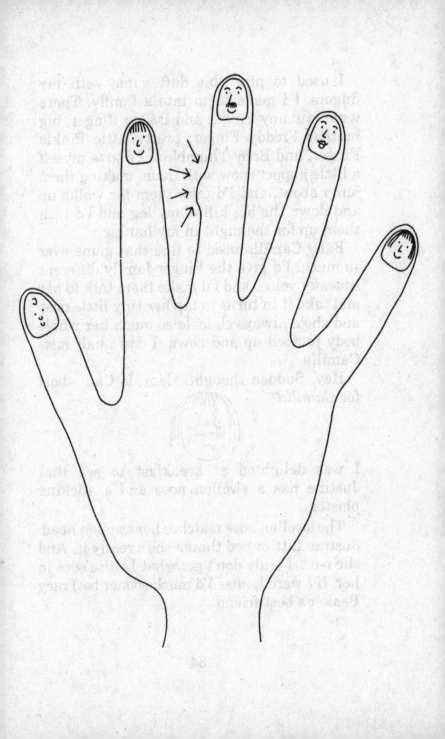

I used to play this daft game with my fingers. I'd make them into a family. There were Mummy Finger and Daddy Finger, big brother Freddy Finger, pretty little Pinkie Finger, and Baby Thumbkin. I'd give myself a little puppet show with them, making them jump about, and I'd take them for walks up and down the big hill of my leg and I'd tuck them up for the night in my hankie.

Baby Camilla used to like that game ever so much. I'd give the Finger family different squeaky voices and I'd make them talk to her and take it in turns to tap her tiny little nose and she'd always chuckle so much her whole body jumped up and down. I don't half miss Camilla.

Hey. Sudden thought. Cam. Is Cam short for *Camilla*?

I was delighted at breakfast to see that Justine has a swollen nose and a sticking plaster.

The swollen nose matches her swollen head. Justine Littlewood thinks she's really it. And she isn't. I truly don't get what Louise sees in her. If *I* were Louise I'd much sooner be Tracy Beaker's best friend.

What really gets me is that I was the one who palled up with Justine first. She turned up at the Home one evening, all down and droopy because her mum had cleared off with some bloke and left Justine and her two little brothers and her dad to get on with it. Only her dad couldn't get on with it, and the kids got taken into care. The brothers got into a short-term foster home because they were still nearly at the baby stage and not too much bother. But Justine didn't get taken on too, because they thought she'd be difficult.

I generally like kids who are difficult. And I thought I liked the look of Justine. And the sound of her. Because after the first droopy evening she suddenly found her tongue and she started sounding off at everyone, getting really stroppy and swearing. She knew even more swear words than I do.

She was like that all week but she shut up on Sunday. Her dad was supposed to see her on Sunday. She was sitting waiting for him right after breakfast, though he wasn't supposed to be coming till eleven o'clock. Eleven came and went. And twelve. And then it was dinnertime and Justine wouldn't eat her chicken. She sat at the window all afternoon, not budging.

My tummy went tight whenever I looked at her. I knew what it was like. I used to sit like that. Not just here. I used to wait at both my crummy foster homes. And the children's homes in between. Waiting for my mum to come.

But now I've got myself sorted out. No more dumb sitting about for me. Because my mum's probably too far away to come on a quick visit. Yeah, that's it, she's probably abroad somewhere, she's always fancied travelling.

She's maybe in France.

Or Spain, she likes sunshine.

What am I thinking of? She'll have gone to the States. Maybe Hollywood. My mum looks so great she'd easily get into the movies.

You can't hop on a bus and visit your daughter when you're hundreds and thousands of miles away in Hollywood, now can you?

All the same, even though I don't sit waiting, I always go a bit tingly when there's a knock at the door. I hold my breath, waiting to see who it is, just in case . . .

So I could understand what old Justine was going through. I didn't try to talk to her because I knew she'd snap my head off, but I sort of sidled up to her and dropped a lollipop on her lap and backed away. It wasn't exactly my lollipop. I'd snaffled several from little Wayne. His dopey mum is younger than Adele and she hasn't got a clue about babies. Whenever she comes she brings Wayne lollipops. Well, they've got sticks, haven't they? We don't want little Wayne giving himself a poke in the eye. And he's normally so drooly that if you add a lot of lolly-lick as well he gets stickier than Superglue. So it's really a kindness to nick his lollies when he's not looking.

'But why did you want to give one to that Justine?' Louise asked. 'She's horrible, Tracy. She barged right into me on the stairs yesterday and she didn't even say sorry, she just called me a very rude word indeed.' Louise whispered it primly.

'Um. Did she really say that?' I said, giggling. 'Oh she's not so bad really. And anyway, I didn't give her the *red* lollipop. I saved that for you.'

'Thanks, Trace,' said Louise, and she beamed at me.

Oh we were like *that* in those days.

I kept an eye on Justine. She didn't budge for a good half hour, letting the lollipop lie in her lap. And then I saw her hand creep out. She unwrapped it and gave it one small suspicious lick, as if I'd poisoned it. But it must have tasted OK because she took another lick, and then another, and then she settled down for a good long suck. Lollipops can be very soothing to the stomach.

She didn't say thank you or anything. And when she eventually had to give up waiting and go to bed she stalked off by herself. But the next day at breakfast she gave me this little nod. So I nodded back and flicked a cornflake in her direction and she flicked one back, and we ended up having this good game of tiddlyflakes and after that we were friends. Not best friends. Louise was my best friend. Ha.

She moaned at first.

'Why do we have to have that Justine hanging round us all the time?' she complained. 'I don't like her, Trace. She's dead tough.'

'Well, I want to be tough too. You've got to be tough. What do you mean, *I'm* tougher than Justine,' I said, sticking my chin out.

'Nutter,' said Louise.

It started to get to me though. I started swearing worse than Justine and Jenny got really mad at me because Maxy started copying me and even little Wayne would come out with a right mouthful when he felt like it.

So then I started the Dare Game. I've always won any dare. Until Justine came along.

I dared her to say the rudest word she could think of when the vicar came on a visit. And she did.

She dared me to go out in the garden stark naked. And I did.

I dared her to eat a worm. And she did.

She dared *me* to eat a worm.

I said that wasn't fair. She couldn't copy my dare. Louise opened her big mouth and said that I hated worms. 'Then I dare her to eat *two* worms,' said Justine. So I did.

I *did*. Sort of. It wasn't my fault they made me sick. I did swallow them first. Justine said I just spat them out straight away but I *didn't*.

I thought hard. I happen to be a crack hand at skateboarding. Justine's not much good at getting her balance and her steering's rotten. So I fixed up this skateboard assault course round the garden, with sloping benches and all sorts. And I dared Justine to have a go. So she did.

She fell over a lot. But she kept getting up and carrying on. So I said she was disqualified. But Louise said Justine should still win the bet if she completed the course. And she did.

Then Justine dared me
to climb the tree
at the end of the garden.
So I did.
It wasn't *my* fault
I didn't get right to
the top. I didn't ask
that stupid Mike to
interfere. But Justine said
I'd lost that dare,
and Louise backed her up.
I couldn't believe my ears.
Louise was *my* friend.

We couldn't do any more dares because Jenny PUT HER FOOT DOWN. You don't argue when she does that.

The next day Justine's famous dad put in an appearance at long last. Justine had gone on and on about how good-looking he was, just like a pop star, and he actually had an evening job singing in pubs, which was why he couldn't be at home to look after her and her brothers. Well, you should have seen him. Starting to go bald. Pot belly. Medallion. He wasn't *quite* wearing a frilly shirt and flares, but almost.

You wouldn't catch me wanting a dad like that. But Justine gave a weird little whoop when she saw him and jumped up into his arms like a great big baby. He took her on some dumb outing and when she got back she was all bubbly and bouncy and showing off this . . . this present he'd bought her.

← whoops!

I don't know why, but I felt really narked at Justine. It was all right when she didn't get a visit, like us lot. But now I kept picking on her and saying silly sniggery things about her dad. And then she burst into tears.

I was a bit shocked. I didn't say anything *that* bad. And I never thought a really tough girl like Justine would ever cry. *I* don't ever cry, no matter what. I mean, my mum hasn't managed to come and visit me for donkey's years and I don't even *have* a dad, but catch me crying.

And then I got another shock. Because Louise turned on me.

'You are horrid, Tracy,' she said. And then she put her arms right round Justine and gave her a big hug. 'Don't take any notice of her. She's just jealous.'

Me, jealous? Of Justine? Of Justine's dopey dumb dad? She had to be joking.

But it didn't look like she was joking. She and Justine went off together, their arms round each other.

I told myself I didn't care. Although I did care a little bit then. And I did wonder if I'd gone over the top with my remarks. I can have a very cutting tongue.

I thought I'd smooth things over at breakfast. Maybe even tell Justine I hadn't really meant any of it. Not actually apologize, of course, but show her that I was sorry. But it was too late. I was left on my own at breakfast. Louise didn't sit next to me in her usual seat. She went and sat at the table by the window – with Justine.

'Hey, Louise,' I called. And then I called again, louder. 'Have you gone deaf or something?' I yelled.

But she could hear me all right. She just wasn't talking to me. She wasn't my best friend any more. She was Justine's.

All I've got is silly squitty twitty Peter Ingham. Oh, maybe he's not so bad. I was writing all this down when there was this tiny tapping at my door. As if some timid little insect was scrabbling away out there. I told this beetle to buzz off because I was busy, but it went on scribble-scrabbling. So eventually I heaved myself off my bed and went to see what it wanted.

'Do you want to play, Tracy?' he said.
'Play?' I said witheringly. 'What do you think I am, Peter Ingham? Some kind of infant? I'm busy writing.' But I'd been writing

so much my whole arm ached and my writing lump was all red and throbbing. Oh, how we writers suffer for our art! It's chronic, it really is.

So I did just wonder if it was time for a little diversion.

'What sort of games do *you* play then, little Peetle-Beetle?'

He blinked a bit and shuffled backwards as if I was about to squash him, but he managed to squeak out something about paper games.

'Paper games?' I said. 'Oh, I see. Do we make a football out of paper and then give it a kick so that it blows away? What fun. Or do we make a dear little teddy out of paper and give it a big hug and squash it flat? Even better.'

Peter giggled nervously. 'No, Tracy, pen and paper games. I always used to play noughts and crosses with my nan.'

'Oh gosh, how incredibly thrilling,' I said.

Beetles don't understand sarcasm.

'Good, *I* like noughts and crosses too,' he said, producing a pencil out of his pocket.

There was no deterring him. So we played paper games after that.

I suppose it passed the time a bit. And now I've just spotted something. Right at the bottom of the page, in teeny tiny beetle writing, there's a little message.

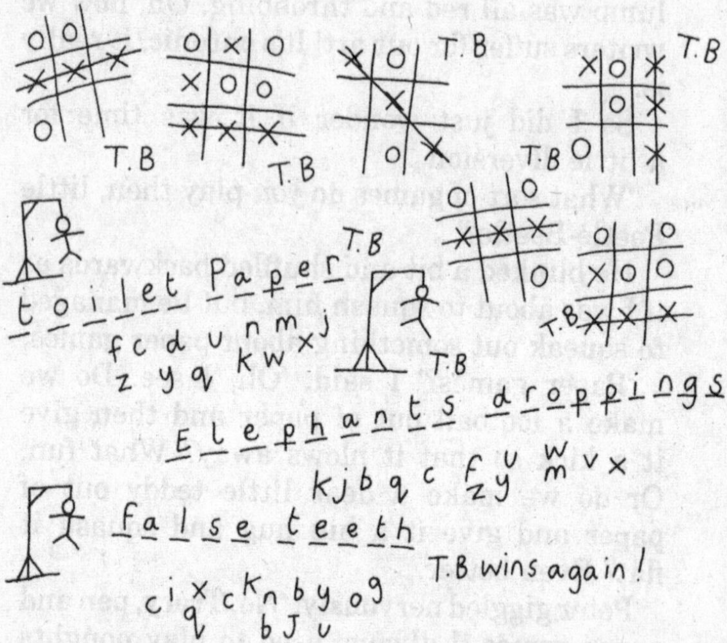

T.B

T.B

T.B

T.B

T.B

T.B

T.B

t o i l e t P a p e r

f c d u n m j
z y q k w x

E l e p h a n t s d r o p p i n g s

k j b q c f u w v x
z y m

f a l s e t e e t h

T.B wins again!

c i x c k n b y o g
q b j u

Justine Littlewood's father

met my nan

Censored!

At the sewage works

he said to her ▨▨▨▨▨▨▨▨▨

I don't half like
you, Tracy.
signed Peter Ingham.

Guess what! I've got a letter!

Not another soppy little message from Peter. A real private letter that came in the post, addressed to Ms Tracy Beaker.

I haven't had many letters just recently. Oh, there have been plenty of letters *about* me. Elaine's got a whole library of files on me. I've had a secret rifle through them and you should just see some of the mean horrid things they say about me. I had a good mind to sue them for libel. Yeah, that would be great. And I'd get awarded all these damages, hundreds of thousands of pounds, and I'd be able to thumb my nose at Justine and Jenny and Elaine and all the others. I'd just clutch my lovely lolly in my hot little hand and go off and . . .

Well, I'd have my own house, right? And I'd employ someone to foster me. But because I'd be paying them, *they'd* have to do everything *I* said. I'd order them to make me a whole birthday cake to myself every single day of the week and they'd just have to jump to it and do so.

I wouldn't let anybody else in to share it with me.

Not even Peter. I had to share my *real* birthday cake with him. And he gave me a nudge and said 'What's the matter, Tracy? Don't you feel well?' just when I'd closed my

eyes tight and was in the middle of making my birthday wish. So it got all muddled and I lost my thread and now if my mum doesn't come for me it's all that Peter Ingham's fault.

Well, maybe it is.

But I'd still let him come round to my house sometimes and we could play paper games. They're quite good fun really, because I always win.

Who else could I have in my house? I could try and get Camilla. I'd look after her. I could get a special playpen and lots of toys. I've always liked the look of all that baby junk. I don't suppose I had much of that sort of thing when I was a baby. Yeah, I could

have a proper nursery in my house and when
Camilla wasn't using it I could muck about in
there, just for a laugh.

I wonder if Camilla remembers me now?
That's the trouble with babies.
I wonder if Cam *is* short for Camilla?
That's who my letter was from.

I was a bit disappointed at first. I thought it was from my mum. I know she's never written to me before but still, when Jenny handed it to me at breakfast I just clutched at the envelope and held it tight and shut my eyes quick because they got suddenly hot and prickly and if I was a snivelly sort of person I might well have cried.

'What's up with Tracy?' the other kids mumbled.

I gave a great swallow and sniff and opened my eyes and said, 'Nothing's up! Look, I've got a letter! A letter from—'

'I think it's maybe from Cam Lawson,' Jenny said, very quickly indeed.

I caught my breath. 'Yeah. Cam Lawson. See that? She's written me my own personal letter. And she's not written to any of you lot. See! She's written to *me*.'

'So what does she say then?'

'Never you mind. It's *private*.'

I went off to read it all by myself. I didn't get around to it for a bit. I was thinking all these dopey things about my mum. And I had a bad attack of hay fever. And I didn't really want to read what Cam Lawson had to say anyway. She saw me having my hairy fit. I was scared she'd think me some sort of loony.

Only the letter was OK.

10 Beech Road
Kingtown

Dear Tracy

    We didn't really get together properly when
I came on my visit. It was a pity because Jenny
told me a bit about you and I liked the sound of
you. She said you're very naughty and you like
writing.

    I'm exactly the opposite. I've
always been very very good. Especially
when I was at school. You wouldn't half
have teased me.

I'm not quite so good now, thank goodness.

    And I hate writing. Because it's what I do
for a living and every day I get up from my cornflakes
and go and sit at my typewriter and my hands clench
into fists and I go cross-eyed staring at the blank
paper - and I think - what a stupid way to earn a
living. Why don't I do something else? Only I'm
useless at everything else so I just have to carry
on with my writing.

    Are you carrying on with your writing? You're
telling your own story? An actual autobiography?
Most girls your age wouldn't have much
to write about, but you're lucky in that
respect because so many different things
have happened to you.

    Good luck with it.

       Yours,

         Cam

Dear Ms Lawson,
              Jenny says that's what I should
call you, Ms Lawson, although you wrote Cam
at the bottom of your letter. What sort of name is
Cam? If you're called Camilla then I think that's
a lovely name and don't see why you want to muck
it up. I had a friend in this other home called
Camilla and she liked her name. I had a special way
of saying it, Ca-miiii-lla, and she'd always
giggle. She was only a baby but very bright.
              Why don't you mind me being naughty?
Actually, its not always my fault that I get
into trouble. People just pick on me. Lots of
people, but I won't name names because I don't
tell tales, not like _some_ people.

Do you like my drawing? I
liked yours, I thought they
were funny. What do you
mean, you hate writing?

Tracy Beaker did this.
Tracy Beaker did that.
Um Tracy Beaker is
awful!

GLUE

I think that's weird when it's what you do. I like writing. I think it's ever so easy. I just start and it goes on and on. The only trouble is that it hurts your hand and you get a big lump on your finger. And ink all over your hand and clothes and paper if some clueless toddler has been chewing on your felt tip.

Are you having trouble writing your article about us? I could help you if you liked. I can tell you anything you need to know about me. And the others. How about it?

Yes I am still writing my autobiography. I like that word. I asked Jenny and she said it's a story about yourself, and that's right, that's exactly what I'm writing. I'd let you have a look at it but it's strictly personal. Don't take any notice of what that moron Justine read out. There are some really good bits, honest.

Yours
From your fellow writer

Tracy Beaker

R.S.V.P

That means you've got to reply.

10 Beech Road.

Dear Tracy,

Thanks for your lovely letter. It made me laugh. Do you know what? I think you're a born writer. I could do with some help on my feature.

Are you around next Saturday morning? Hope to see you then. Cam. I hate Camilla. I used to get teased rotten at school for having such a soppy name.

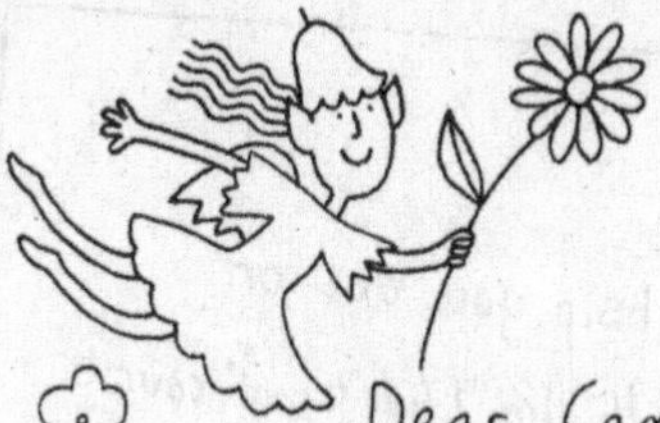

The dumping Ground.

Dear Camilla,

It's not a soppy name. You've got to be proud of it. You want to try having a name like Tracy Beaker. Excuse this ccummy writing paper. Jenny lent me the first lot but she says I'm costing her a small fortune in paper and can't I give it a rest. So I borrowed this from one of the little ones. Isn't it yucky? I know.

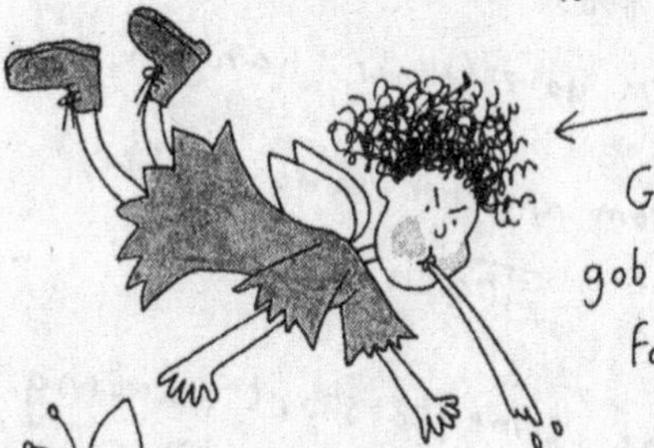

This is Goblinda the Goblin and she's going to gob all over these daft fairies.

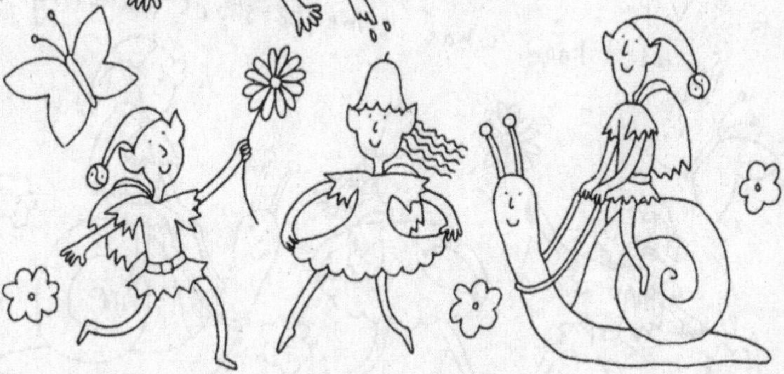

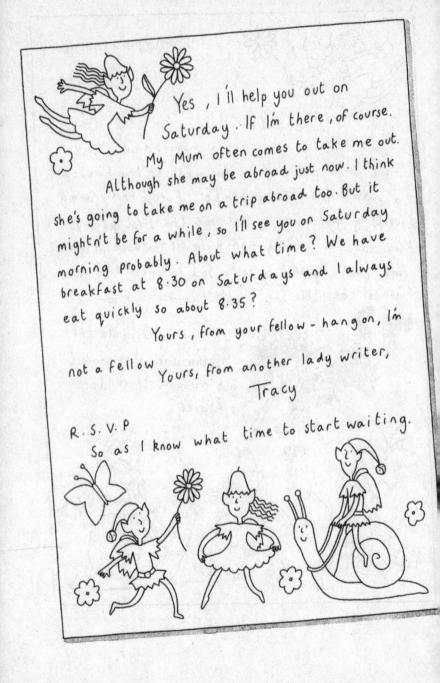

Yes, I'll help you out on Saturday. If I'm there, of course.

My Mum often comes to take me out. Although she may be abroad just now. I think she's going to take me on a trip abroad too. But it mightn't be for a while, so I'll see you on Saturday morning probably. About what time? We have breakfast at 8.30 on Saturdays and I always eat quickly so about 8.35?

Yours, from your fellow – hang on, I'm not a fellow Yours, from another lady writer,

Tracy

R. S. V. P

So as I know what time to start waiting.

Dear Sister Writer,

See you Saturday morning. 8·35

I look like this at 8·35.

10 Beech Road

How about 10·35?

Cam. Sorry Camilla. Ugh!

Put her in a story.

8·35 impossible.

P.S. I love Goblinda.

Imagine staying in your bed half the morning. She is lazy. And she was late even then. It was 10.41 before she turned up. I'd practically given her up. She's supposed to be a professional writer and yet she can't even keep an appointment on time.

She's pretty hopeless if you ask me. She didn't half muck up this morning. I'd got it all worked out. I was ready to fill her in on all the facts. Mostly about me, of course. But I thought maybe she might fancy interviewing Peter too, to balance things up. A girl's point of view, and a boy's. No need to bother with any of the others.

Cam's got this dinky little tape recorder and after just one minute of instruction I mastered all the mechanism and had great fun fast-forwarding and rewinding and playing back. I had a little go first, trying out all my different accents, doing my Australian G'day routine and my American gangster and my special Donald Duck, but then I decided we'd better get down to business and as I'm not the sort of girl to hog the limelight I said Peter could go first.

He backed away from the tape recorder as if it was a loaded gun.

'Don't be so silly, Peter. Just act normal and speak into it.'

'What shall I say?' Peter squeaked.

I sighed impatiently. 'Just tell Cam your life story.'

'But I haven't got a story. I couldn't think of anything to put when Elaine gave me that book,' said Peter. 'I lived with my nan. And she died. So I came here. That's all there is.'

'That's OK, Peter. Don't let Tracy bully you into it. You don't have to say anything,' said Cam.

'What a cheek! I'm not a bully. Huh, *I* was the kid who always *got* bullied. This other Home I was in, there was this huge great teenage bloke, and he was a really tough skinhead and he had these bovver boots and I filled them up with custard for a joke and he didn't see the funny side of it

113

and yet he didn't half look hilarious, all this frothy yellow liquid squishing up his trouser legs – so anyway, from then on my name was mud, and he really had it in for me. The things he used to do!'

I was about to launch into a long account but typical typical that Justine Littlewood came barging over.

'It's not fair, Miss. You're letting that stupid Tracy show off like mad, and you're not giving any of us a go.'

'You shut your face, blabbermouth,' I said. 'She's not come to see you lot. She's come to see *me*. A strictly private appointment. So clear off. Isn't that right, Cam?'

'Well. Yes, I've come to talk to you, Tracy. But we could all have a go on the tape recorder for a bit,' she said.

What a gutless creep she is. She was there just to see *me*. We had a proper business appointment. All she had to do was tell Justine and the others to buzz off. It wouldn't have mattered if Peter stayed, because he's not really any bother. But the others! It was useless. Practically the whole morning was wasted. She let them all muck around on the tape recorder and then some of the littlies wanted another go drawing with her Mickey Mouse pen, and then Jenny came in with coffee for Cam and coke for us and it was like some big party. Only I didn't feel like the birthday girl. I felt squeezed out to the edge again.

After a bit I stomped off. I kept looking back over my shoulder and I thought she didn't even notice. But then she sidled up. She still had baby Becky on one hip and little Wayne clinging to her leg like a limpet. She gave me a dig in the back with her Mickey Mouse pen.

'Hey,' she said softly. 'Shall we get started on your interview now, Tracy?'

'Well, you've got all these other kids. Why waste your time with me?' I said acidly. 'I mean, I'm only the one you were *supposed* to see.'

'Tell you what. Let's go up to your room. Just you and me. How about it?'

'OK,' I said, yawning and shrugging. 'If you really want. I've gone off the idea now. But if you insist. Just for a minute or two.'

It took her a while to dump the baby and prise Wayne away, and then all the others kept clustering around, saying it wasn't fair. So do you know what she did? She said they could do interviews on her tape recorder. And she put *Justine* in charge of it.

'You aren't half making a mistake there, Cam. You're crazy. They'll wreck it in two minutes,' I said.

'No they won't. Justine will work it. And everyone take a two-minute turn. Introduce yourselves first, and then say whatever you want. But don't worry, Peter, you don't have to.'

'You are stark staring mad,' I said. 'Look, if anyone's in charge of that tape recorder it's got to be me. I'm the only one who knows how to work it properly.'

'Well, show Justine,' said Cam. 'Then she'll be able to work it too.'

'I'm not showing *her*,' I said. But in the end I did. And of course Justine was clueless and didn't catch on and I kept sighing and groaning and she got narked and gave me a push and I clenched my fist ready to give her a thump but Cam got in between us and said, 'Look, I'll run through it. Here's the record button, Justine, right?' and *eventually* Justine got the hang of it. I don't know why she's called Littlewood. Little*brain* would be far more appropriate.

Then Cam and I went up to my room and left them to it.

'You thought you'd found a way of getting Justine and me to make friends,' I said. 'But, ha-ha, it didn't work, did it? Because we're always going to be deadly enemies.'

Cam laughed at me. She laughed at the notice taped on my bedroom door too.

THIS ROOM BELONGS TO
TRACY BEAKER
STRICTLY PRIVATE
KEEP OUT ON PAIN OF DEATH.
AND IT WILL BE A <u>VERY</u> PAINFUL
DEATH TOO.

'It's OK. You can come in. You're my guest,' I said, opening the door for her.

My room looked a bit of a tip actually. I hadn't got round to making the bed and the floor was littered with socks and pyjama tops and bits of biscuit and pencil sharpenings, so she had to pick her way through. She didn't make a big thing of it though. She looked at all the stuff I've got pinned to my noticeboard, and she nodded a bit and smiled.

'Is that your mum?' Cam asked.

'Isn't she lovely? You'd really think she was a film star, wouldn't you? I think she maybe *is* a film star now. In Hollywood. And she'll be jetting over to see me soon. Maybe she'll take me back with her, and I'll get to be a film star too. A child star. The marvellous movie moppet, Tracy Beaker. Yeah. That would be great, eh?'

I spun around with a great grin, doing a cutsie-pie curtsey – and Cam caught on straight away and started clapping and acting like an adoring fan.

'I hope you're still going to be a writer too,' she said. 'Have you done any more about Goblinda?'

'Give us a chance. I've been too busy doing my autobiography,' I said.

'I suppose this autobiography of yours is strictly private?' Cam asked, sounding a bit wistful.

'Of course it is,' I said. But then I hesitated. Elaine the Pain has seen bits of it. And Louise and Littlebrain. And I did show a bit to Peter actually, just to show him how much I'd done. So why shouldn't I show a bit to Cam too? As she's a sort of friend.

So I let her have a few peeps. I had to be a bit careful, because some of the stuff I've written about her isn't exactly flattering. She came across a description of her by accident, but she didn't take offence. She roared with laughter.

'You really should be the one writing this article about children in care, Tracy, not me. I think you'd make a far better job of it.'

'Yes, have you made a start on this article yet?'

She fidgeted a bit. 'Not really. It's difficult. You see, this magazine editor wants a very touching sentimental story about all these sad sweet vulnerable little children that will make her readers reach for a wad of Kleenex.'

'Yeah, that's the right approach.'

'Oh come off it, Tracy. None of you lot are at all *sweet*. You're all gutsy and stroppy and spirited. I want to write what you're really like but it won't be the sort of thing the editor wants.'

'And it won't be the sort of thing *I* want either. You've got to make me sound sweet, Cam! No-one will want me otherwise. I've gone past my sell-by date already. It gets hopeless when you get older than five or six. You've stopped being a cute little toddler and started to be difficult. And I'm not pretty either so people won't take one look at my photo and start cooing. And then it's not like I'm up for adoption so people can't ever make me their little girl, not properly.'

'You're not up for adoption because you've still got your mum?'

'Exactly. And like I said, she'll be coming for me soon, but meanwhile I'd like to live in a proper homey home instead of this old dump. Otherwise I'll get institutionalized.'

Cam's eyebrows go up.

'I know what it means and all. I've heard Elaine and some of the other social workers going on about it. It's when you get so used to living in an institution like this that you never learn how to live in a proper home. And when you get to eighteen you can't cope and you don't know how to do your own shopping or cooking or anything. Although I can't see me ever having that problem. I bet I could cope right this minute living on my own. They'd just have to bung me the lolly and I'd whizz off down the shops and have a whale of a time.'

'I bet you would,' said Cam.

Then Maxy started scratching at my door

and whining and complaining. I told him to push off, because Cam and I were In Conference, but he didn't take any notice.

'Miss, Miss, it's not fair, them big girls won't let me have a go on the tape, I want a go, Miss, you tell them to let me have a go, they're playing they're pop stars, Miss, and *I* want a go.'

Cam smiled and sighed, looking at her watch.

'I'd better go back downstairs. I've got to be going in a minute anyway.'

'Oh that's not fair! Aren't you staying? You can have lunch with us lot, Jenny won't mind, and it's hamburgers on Saturday.'

'No, I'm meeting someone for lunch in the town.'

'Oh. Where are you going then?'

'Well, we'll probably have a drink and then we'll have a salad or something. My friend fusses about her figure.'

'Who wants boring old salad? If I was having lunch out I'd go to McDonald's. I'd have a Big Mac and french fries and a strawberry milkshake. See, I'm not the slightest bit institutionalized, am I?'

'You've been to McDonald's then?'

'Oh, heaps of times,' I said. And then I paused. 'Well, not actually *inside*. I was fostered with this boring family, Julie and Ted, and I kept on at them to take me, but they said it was junk food. And I said all their boring brown beans and soggy veggy stews were the *real* junk because they looked like someone had already eaten them and sicked them up and – well, anyway, they never took me.'

'No wonder,' said Cam, grinning.

'I am allowed to go out to lunch from here, you know.'

'Are you?'

'Yes. Any day. And tell you what, I really will work on that article for you. I could work on it this week and show you what I've done. And we could discuss it. Over lunch. At McDonald's. Hint, hint, hint.'

Cam smacked the side of her head as if a great thought has just occurred to her.

'Hey, Tracy! Would you like to come out with me to McDonald's next week?'

'Yes please!' I pause. 'Really? You're not kidding?'

'Really. Next Saturday. I'll come and pick you up about twelve, OK?'

'I'll be waiting.'

And so I shall. I'd better send her a letter too, just in case she forgets.

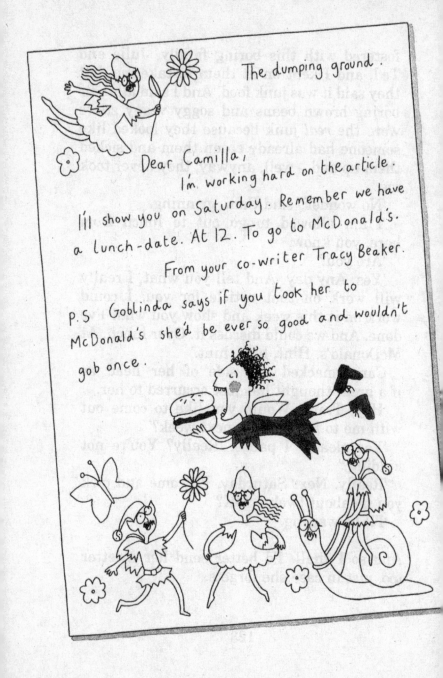

The dumping ground.

Dear Camilla,
          I'm working hard on the article.
I'll show you on Saturday. Remember we have
a lunch-date. At 12. To go to McDonald's.
          From your co-writer Tracy Beaker.

P.S Goblinda says if you took her to
McDonald's she'd be ever so good and wouldn't
gob once.

I know she said twelve o'clock. And she's not exactly the most punctual of people. She mightn't get here till ten past. Even twenty or half past. So why am I sitting here staring out of the window when we've only just had breakfast?

I hate waiting. It really gets on my nerves. I can't concentrate on anything. Not even my writing. And I haven't done any writing in this book all week because I've been so busy with my article for Cam. I've got it all finished now and even though I say it myself I've done a really great job. She can just bung it at her editor and no-one will be any the wiser. I should really get the whole fee for it myself. But I'm very generous. I'll share fifty fifty with Cam, because she's my friend.

Old Pete's my friend too. We've been bumping into each other in the middle of the night this week, on a sheet sortie. Mostly we just had a little whisper but last night I found him all huddled up and soggy because he'd had a nightmare about his nan. Strangely enough, I'd had a nightmare about my mum and it had brought on a bad attack of my hay fever. Normally I like to keep to myself at such moments as some stupid ignorant twits think my red eyes and runny nose are because I've been crying. And I never *ever* cry, no matter what.

But I knew Peter wouldn't tease me so I huddled down beside him for a bit and when I felt him shivering I put my arm round him and told him he was quite possibly my best friend ever.

He's just come up to me now and asked if I want to play paper games. Yeah, it might pass the time.

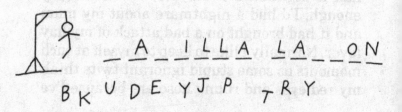

_ A _ I L L A _ L A _ _ O N

B K U D E Y J P T R Y

Oh charming! Peter and I had just got started and I was about to win the first game when Elaine the Pain comes buzzing in. She's here dumping off some boring new kid and now she wants to have a little chat with Peter.

'Well, tough, Elaine, because *I'm* having a little chat with Peter right now,' I said.

'Now now Tracy,' said Elaine.

'Yes, *now*,' I said.

Elaine bared her teeth at me. That smile means she'd really like to give me a clip around the ear but she's going to make allowances for me.

'I expect you're feeling a bit het up this morning, Tracy, because of this writer coming to take you out. Jenny's told me all about it. It'll be a lovely treat for you.'

'You bet. And it'll be a lovely treat for her too because I've written this article for her.'

'Well, I might have a little treat up my sleeve for Peter here,' Elaine said, and she shuffled him off into a corner and started talking to him earnestly.

She's still talking to him. She's keeping her voice down. But I can have very large waggly ears when I want. Elaine's going on about these people she knows. An older couple whose children have all grown up. And now they're a bit lonely. They'd like to look after

127

someone. A little boy. Maybe a little boy just like Peter.

So that's it. Little Peetie-Weetie is obviously going to get fostered and live Happily Ever After.

Well, that's good, isn't it? Because he's my best friend.

No, it's bad, because he won't be able to be my best friend any more if he goes off and gets himself fostered.

And it's not fair. He's hardly been here any time. I've been here ages and ages and no-one ever wants to foster me now.

Still, who wants to be fostered by some boring older couple anyway? Older might mean really ancient. And crabby. And strict. They'd never wear jeans or write funny letters or take Peter to McDonald's.

I wish Cam would hurry up and come for me. Although it's nowhere near time. It's daft me sitting here by the window like this. Waiting.

Justine is hovering behind me. I think she's waiting for her dad. I hope she won't tell him about the little accident to her Mickey Mouse clock. He might come and beat me up. Even though the clock's all mended now. Jenny took it in to this shop and they sorted it. I was glad to see old Mickey tick-tocking round and round again. Justine caught me looking and she gave me this great fierce push that nearly knocked me over and told me that if I so much as touched her clock again she'd duff me up good and proper. Honestly! My fists clenched and I was all set to have a real go at her because no-one talks to Tracy Beaker like that, but then I remembered my lunch date. Jenny isn't best pleased with me at the moment. If I got into a punch-up with Justine then she mightn't let me go out with Cam.

So I Kept Calm. I smiled at Justine in a superior sort of way.

'Really Justine, do you always have to resort to violence?' I said.

My superior willpower was wasted on Justine. She just thought I was chicken.

'Cowardy cowardy custard,' she's mumbling under her breath now. 'Tracy Beaker's got no bottle.'

I shan't take any notice of her. I shall just sit here writing. And waiting. It's not *that* long now. Only it seems like for ever.

I used to sit like this. When I waited for my mum. I wonder when she will come. I had that awful dream about her. I was out having lunch with Cam in McDonald's and it was really great and we were having a smashing time together when I looked up at the clock and saw it had gone one o'clock, and

it suddenly rang a terrible bell in my head, and I remembered that my mum was coming to take me to lunch at one o'clock, and I just went panic panic panic.

I charged off to try to get back to the Home in time and I got a bus but they chucked me off because I didn't have enough money and then I ran into Aunty Peggy and she chased after me to give me a good smacking and Julie and Ted tripped me up and Justine caught me and threw me in a river and I couldn't swim and I was drowning . . . and then I woke up. Wet.

So OK, I know it was only a dopey old nightmare. But what if it was some kind of *premonition*??? What if my mum really comes for me today and I miss her because I'm having lunch with Cam?

I'll have to talk to Elaine.

Well, I've talked. Sort of.

'Can I have a little chat, Elaine?' I said.

'Tracy. I'm still having a little chat with Peter.'

'You've *had* a little chat with Peter. Correction. You've had an extremely long and boring endless conversation with him. And you're my social worker just as much as his. So could you *please* come and have a little chat with me. It's sort of urgent.'

Elaine sighed. She ruffled Peter's hair and gave him a little chuck under the chin. Then she came over to me at long last.

'What is it then, Tracy?'

I swallowed, not sure how to put it.

'Tracy, are you just winding me up?' said Elaine.

'No! It's just ... Look, about my mum. She doesn't know I'm here, does she?'

'Well. No, I don't think so.'

'But if she wanted to find me she could, couldn't she?'

I said it in a whisper but Justine heard.

131

'Who'd ever want to come looking for you, Tracy Beaker?' she said.

'You shut your mouth!'

Justine pulled a hideous face and Louise giggled. Then she tugged at Justine's sleeve.

'Come on. Let's see what that new girl's doing. She's got two whole suitcases with her, so she must have heaps of clothes.'

But Justine wanted to stay at the window so Louise wandered off by herself. I knew Justine was still listening for all she was worth (honestly, some people have no decency whatsoever) but I had to keep on asking Elaine.

'If my mum wanted she could go round to that old children's home. And they could tell her where I am now, couldn't they?'

'Yes, of course they would,' said Elaine. 'Don't worry, Tracy. Each time you get moved on somewhere else, there's a special record kept. So if your mum wants to see you then it's easy. They look up your name and file number and find your present address.'

'Good,' I said.

'What's up, Tracy? You still look a bit worried.'

'I'm OK.'

Only I don't feel OK. What if my mum does come today? And I'm out having lunch with someone else? Will she wait for me? Or

132

will she get fidgety and fed up and zoom off again? And I'll get back here and Jenny will say, 'Oh, by the way, Tracy, your mum called when you were out, but she couldn't wait for you. She was all set to take you back to Hollywood with her but she had this plane to catch so she couldn't hang about.'

What am I going to do?

Maybe she won't come today. She hasn't ever come before. And yet, what if she did? I *wish* I hadn't had that dream. Dreams *can* come true.

I feel sick. Maybe I don't really want to go to McDonald's after all.

See that? It's real blood.

I'm not going to get to go to McDonald's now, whether I want to or not. I've had a fight. I'm in the Quiet Room.

This is how it happened. I went over to Peter. I whispered in his ear.

'Would you like to go to McDonald's with Cam?'

Peter scrunched up his neck because my whispers can be a bit tickly.

'You mean, go with you?'

133

'No. Go instead of me. I've kind of gone off the idea. It's OK, I'll tell Cam when she comes. She quite likes you, so she won't mind taking you instead.'

Peter looked worried.

'I can't, Tracy. I'm going out too. With these people.'

'What, with this boring older couple?' I said.

Elaine raised her eyebrows at me but I took no notice.

'I bet they won't take you to McDonald's,' I said.

'Why don't *you* want to go, Tracy?' Elaine asked. 'I thought you were so looking forward to it.'

'Yes, but ... I want to stay here. Just in case.'

Elaine is a pain but she's also quite quick at putting two and two together.

'Tracy, I don't think your mum will be coming today,' she said quietly.

'Oh. I know that. Only I had this dream. She did in the dream.'

'Yes, I'm sure she did. And I expect it was a lovely dream but—'

'No, it was a perfectly foul dream because I wasn't here to see her and—'

'And you woke up blubbing with a soaking wet bed, *baby*,' Justine muttered.

134

'I told you to shut *up*,' I said, getting really riled.

'I'd go out with your writer friend, Tracy,' said Elaine.

'Mm. Well. I'm not sure I really want to now, anyway.' I glare at Peter. 'Why do you have to be seeing this boring old couple today, eh? You could see them any old time. You go and have a Big Mac with Cam.'

Peter wriggled. Elaine put her hand on his shoulder. He looked up at her and then at me.

'Sorry, Tracy. I want to meet them. Aunty Vi and Uncle Stanley.'

'Of course you want to meet them, Peter. And Tracy is going to meet her writer,' said Elaine.

'No, I'm not.'

'*I'd* go,' said Justine. 'Only I can't, because of my dad. I'm going out to lunch with him.'

'You were supposed to be going out with him last Saturday. Only he never turned up,' I said.

'OK, but he does come *sometimes*. Not like your famous mum. She's never ever ever come for you,' said Justine.

'Oh yes she has!' I yelled. 'She's come for me lots of times. She's going to come and take me away for good, we're going to Hollywood

135

together and – will you stop *laughing* at me, you great big pig.'

'You're so stupid,' Justine gasped. 'Your mum's not a film star. Louise told me about your mum. She's nothing. And she's never coming for you. She hasn't been near you since you were little. I bet she's forgotten all about you. Or she's had heaps of other kids and doesn't want to think about that boring ugly Tracy ever again.'

So I hit her. And I kept on hitting her. And I don't care. I've made her nose bleed again. She's hurt me a bit too, but I don't care. And now I'm stuck in the Quiet Room and it's gone twelve and one of the other kids will get to go out to lunch with Cam instead of me and I don't care. At least it won't be Justine.

Maybe my mum *will* come.

There's someone outside the door. It's opening. *Is it Mum???*

136

No. It wasn't Mum. It never is. It was Cam,
of course.

I took one look at Cam and burst into
tears. Well, I would have done, if I was a
crying sort of person.

'Oh dear,' said Cam. 'I don't seem to have
a very good effect on you, Tracy.'

She sat right down on the floor beside
me, waiting for me to quieten down a bit.
Then she dug in the pocket of her jeans and
found a crumpled tissue. She passed it to me
and I mopped up my hay fever.

'Now,' said Cam. 'What do you want to do?'

'I haven't got any choice, have I? I'm
stuck here.'

'No you're not. You can still come out
to lunch with me. I've asked Jenny. Elaine
explained why you got upset.'

137

'She doesn't know! I hate the idea of you lot all blabbing away about me,' I said fiercely.

'Yes, it must get a bit annoying,' said Cam. 'Still, at least it means you're the centre of everyone's attention. Here, you've still got a runny nose. Good job you weren't wearing your make-up this time.'

'Are you laughing at me?'

'Just a little tease. Coming?'

'You bet.'

Only I *still* felt bothered about my mum, even though I knew it was silly. I knew she almost definitely wouldn't be coming. I knew deep deep down that Justine was maybe right about her. But I still worried.

'My mum,' I mumbled.

'You're scared she'll come and you won't be here?' said Cam. 'OK. Tell you what we'll do. You can phone home when we're out. To check she's not arrived. And if she *has* I'll whisk you straight back. How about that?'

'That sounds great,' I said.

So Cam and I went off together for our lunch appointment after all. She's got this ancient grass-green Citroën which made a bit of a change from the Minivan.

'My mum wouldn't be seen dead in this sort of naff car,' I said. 'She drives a Cadillac you know.'

'Mm,' said Cam.

I squinted at her. 'You're just nodding to be nice to me, aren't you?' I said. 'You don't really believe my mum's got her own Cadillac.'

Cam looked at me. 'Do you believe it, Tracy?'

I thought for a bit. 'Sometimes.'

Cam nodded again.

'And sometimes I know I'm sort of making it up,' I mumbled. 'Do you mind that? Me telling lies?'

'I make things up all the time when I write stories. I don't mind a bit,' said Cam.

'I've got that article with me. I've written it all. You won't have to bother with a thing. Shall I read a bit to you? You'll be really impressed, I bet you will. I think I've done a dead professional job.'

So I started reading it to her.

'You can see the signs of suffering on little Tracy Beaker's elfin face. This very very intelligent and extremely pretty little girl has been grievously treated when in so-called Care. Her lovely talented young mother had to put her in a home through no fault of her own, and in fact she might soon be coming for her lovely little daughter, but until then dear little Tracy Beaker needs a foster family. She is deprived and abused in the dump of a children's home— Why are you laughing, Cam?'

'Abused?' Cam spluttered.

'Look at my hand. My knuckles. That's blood, you know.'

'Yes, and you got it bouncing your fist up and down on poor Justine's nose,' said Cam. 'You're the one who deprives and abuses all the others in your Home.'

'Yes, but if I put that no-one will want me, will they?'

'I don't know,' said Cam. 'If I were choosing, I'd maybe go for a really naughty girl. It might be fun.'

I looked at her. And went on looking at her. And my brain started going tick tick tick.

I was mildly distracted when we got to McDonald's. I ate a Big Mac and a large portion of french fries, and washed it down with a strawberry milkshake. So did Cam. Then she had a coffee and I had another milkshake. And then we sat back, stuffed. We both had to undo our belts a bit.

I got out my article again and showed her some more, but she got the giggles all over again.

'I'll give myself hiccups,' she said weakly. 'It's no use, Tracy. I think it's great, but they'll never print it. You can't say those sort of things.'

'What, that Tracy Beaker is brilliant and the best child ever? It's true!'

'Maybe! But you can't say all the other things, about Justine and Louise and the rest.'

'But they're true too.'

'No, they're not true at all. I've met them. I like them. And you certainly can't say those things about Jenny and Mike and your social worker and all the others. You'd get sued for libel.'

'Well, you do better then,' I said huffily. 'What would you put?'

'I don't know. Maybe I don't want to do the article now anyway. I think I'd sooner stick to my stories, and blow the money.'

'That's not a very professional approach,' I said sternly. 'Maybe you ought to give up writing. Maybe you ought to do some job that gives you a whacking great allowance. Looking after someone. You get an allowance for that.'

Cam raised her eyebrows.

'I can barely look after myself,' she said.

'Well then. You need someone to look after you for a bit,' I said. 'Someone like me.'

'Tracy.' Cam looked me straight in the eye. 'No. Sorry. *I* can't foster you.'

'Yes, you can.'

'Stop it. We can't start this. I'm not in any position to foster you.'

'Yes you are. You don't need to be married, you know. Single women can foster kids easy-peasy.'

'I'm single and I want to stay single. No husband. And *no kids*.'

'Good. I hate other kids. Especially boring little babies. You won't ever get broody, will you, Cam?'

'No fear. Holding that little Wayne was enough to douse any maternal urges for ever,' said Cam.

'So it could be just you and me.'

'No!'

'Think about it.'

Cam laughed. 'You aren't half persistent, girl! OK, OK, I'll think about it. That's all. Right?'

'Right,' I say, and I tap her hand triumphantly. 'Can I phone home now? I sound like E.T., don't I? We've got through two videos of that already. So, can T.B. phone home? Only she doesn't have any change.'

Cam gave me ten pence and I went to the phone by the Ladies and gave Jenny a buzz. My heart did thump a bit when I was waiting for her to answer. I felt a little bit sad when she told me that Mum hadn't come. Even though that was the answer I was really expecting.

But I had other things to fuss about now. I whizzed back to Cam.

'Well? Have you had your think? Is it

143

OK? Will you take me on?' I asked eagerly.

'Hey, hey! I've got to think about this for ages and ages. And then I'm almost certain it's still going to be no.'

'*Almost* certain. But not absolutely one hundred percent.'

'Mm. What about you? Are you absolutely one hundred percent sure you'd like me to foster you?'

'Well. I'd sooner you were rich. And posh and that, so that I could get on in the world.'

'I think you'll get on in the world without my help, Tracy.'

'No, I need you, Cam.'

I looked straight at her. And she looked straight at me.

'We still hardly know each other,' she said.

'Well, if we lived together we would get to know each other, wouldn't we, Cam? Camilla. That sounds classier. I want my foster mum to sound dead classy.'

'Oh Tracy, give it a rest. Me, classy? And I told you, I can't stick Camilla. I used to get teased. And that's what my mum always called me.' She pulled a face.

I was shocked by her tone and her expression.

'Don't you . . . don't you *like* your mum?' I said.

'Not much.'

144

'Why? Did she beat you up or something?'

'No! No, she just bossed me about. And my father too. They tried to make me just like them and when I wanted to be different they couldn't accept it.'

'So don't you see them any more?'

'Not really. Just at Christmas.'

'Good, so they'll give me Christmas presents, won't they, if I'm their foster grandchild?'

'Tracy! Look, it really wouldn't work. It wouldn't work for heaps of practical reasons, let alone anything else. I haven't got room for you. I live in this tiny flat.'

'I'm quite small. I don't take up much space.'

'But my flat's really minute, you should see it.'

'Oh great! Can we go there now?'

'I didn't mean— ' Cam began – but she laughed again. 'OK, we'll go round to my flat. Only I told Jenny I'd take you back to the Home after lunch.'

'T.B. can phone home again, can't she?'

'I suppose so. Tell Jenny I'll get you back by teatime.'

'Can't I come to tea with you too? Please?'

'Tell you what. We could pretend to be posh ladies just to please you and have afternoon tea. About four. Although I don't know how either of us could possibly eat another thing.

And then I'll take you back to the Home by five. Right?'

'What about supper? And look, I could stay the night, we're allowed to do that, and I don't need pyjamas, I could sleep in my underwear, and I needn't bother about washing things, I often don't wash back at the Home—'

'Great! Well, if you ever lived with me – and I said *if*, Tracy – then you'd wash all right. Now don't carry on. Five. Back at the Home. That'll be quite enough for today.'

I decided to give in. I sometimes sense I can only push so far.

I phoned, and Cam spoke to Jenny for a bit too.

'T.B.'s phoned home twice now. Like E.T. Do you know what E.T. got?' I said hopefully.
'Smarties.'

'You'll be in the Sunday papers tomorrow, Tracy. THE GIRL WHOSE STOMACH EXPLODED,' said Cam.

But she bought me Smarties all the same. Not a little tube, a great big packet.

'Wow! Thanks,' I said, tucking in.

'They're not just for you. Take them back and share them with all the others.'

'Oh! I don't want to waste them.'

'You're to share them, greedyguts.'

'I don't mind sharing them with Peter. Or Maxy. Or the babies.'

146

'Share them with everybody. Including Justine.'

'Hmm!'

She stopped off at another shop too. A baker's. She made me wait outside. She came out carrying a cardboard box.

'Is that cakes for our tea?'

'Maybe.'

'Yum yum. I'm going to like living with you, Cam.'

'Stop it now. Look Tracy, I seem to have got a bit carried away. I like seeing you and I hope we can go out some other Saturdays—'

'Great! To McDonald's? Is that a promise?'

'That really is a promise. But about fostering ... I'd hate you to build your hopes up, Tracy. Let's drop the subject now and just be friends, OK?'

'You could be my friend *and* my foster mum.'

'You're like a little dog with a bone. You just won't let go, will you?'

'Woof woof!'

147

I'm getting good at making her laugh. I like her. Quite a lot. Not as much as my mum, of course. But she'll do, until my mum comes to get me.

Her flat came as a bit of a shock, mind you. It really is weeny. And ever so shabby. It's in far worse nick than the Home. And you should see her bedroom. She leaves her pyjamas on the floor too!

Still, once I get to live there I'll get her sorted out. Help her make a few improvements.

'Show me your books then,' I said, going over to the shelves. 'Did you write all this lot?'

'No, no! Just the ones on the bottom shelf. I don't think you'll find them very exciting, Tracy.'

She was dead right there. I flicked through one, but I couldn't find any pictures, or any funny bits, or even any rude bits. I'll have to get her to write some better books or she'll never make enough money to keep me in the style to which I want to become accustomed.

Maybe I'll have to hurry up and get my own writing published. I got Cam to give me a good long go on her typewriter.

It took me a while to get the hang of it. But eventually I managed to tap out a proper letter. I left it tucked away on Cam's desk for her to find later.

```
    DEAR CAM,  I WILL BE THE BESTEST FOSTER
CHILD EVER.  YOU'LL SEE.  WITH LOVE FROM
TRACY BEAKER, THE GIRL WHOSE STOMACH DIDN'T
EXPLODE.
```

It did nearly though. Guess what she bought for tea! A birthday cake, quite a big one, with jam and cream inside. The top

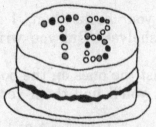

was just plain white, but she took some of my
Smarties and spelt out T.B. on the top.

'So that it's all my cake,' I said happily.

'Aren't I going to get a slice?' asked Cam.

'Oh yes. Of course. But I don't have to
share it with anyone else. I had to share my
proper birthday cake with Peter, wasn't that
mean!'

'I thought Peter's your friend.'

'Well. He is. But still. You don't want
to share your birthday cake even with your
bestest friend ever,' I said.

Only I started thinking about it all the
time I was chomping my way through my
first great big slice. And my second slice with
extra jam and cream. And my third weeny
slice. And my nibbles at a bit of icing.

'This is much better than that birthday
cake at the Home, you know,' I said.

'Good.'

'Peter's gone out with this dumb sounding
old auntie and uncle today,' I said.

'Has he?'

'But I bet they won't take him to Mc-Donald's. Or buy him his own special cake.'

'Maybe not.'

'Well, seeing as we are friends, Peter and me, and we share a birthday, and we shared that other birthday cake – maybe we *ought* to share this one too,' I said. 'Shall I take a slice back for my friend Peter?'

'I think that would be a good idea,' said Cam. 'I'll wrap up a slice for Peter. And another slice for you. Just so long as you promise me you won't throw up all night.'

'Of course I won't. Here, can I do the cutting this time? Because if this is like a birthday cake I get a wish, don't I?'

So Cam gave me the knife and I closed my eyes and wished really really hard.

'I bet you can't guess what I wished,' I said to Cam.

'I bet I can,' said Cam.

'I'll tell you if you like.'

'Oh no. You're supposed to keep birthday cake wishes secret,' said Cam.

I pulled a little face at her. Then I thought.

'Here, if this is a sort of birthday, then it's a pity there aren't any presents too.' I paused. 'Hint hint hint.'

'Do you know what you are, Tracy Beaker? Absolutely shameless.'

But it worked!

Cam looked all round her room and stared for a while at her bookshelves. I thought I was going to end up with a boring old book. But it was much much better. She went to her desk and picked up her Mickey Mouse pen.

'Here we are, Tracy. Happy Unbirthday,' she said, and she pressed the pen into my hand.

Just for a moment I was lost for words. And that doesn't happen very often to me. I was scared I might even get another attack of my hay fever. But I managed to grin and give her the thumbs up sign and show her that I was ever so pleased.

We got back to the Home at five. On the dot. Trust her to be punctual at the wrong time. I made a bit of a fuss on the doorstep. I sort of clung a bit. It was just that I was enjoying myself so much that I wanted to go *on* enjoying myself. That's not being difficult, is it?

But it's still OK. She's coming next Saturday. She's promised. Twelve o'clock. We have a date, me and my future foster mum. I'm going to make that wish come true.

It took me a bit of time to calm down after we'd said goodbye. I missed out on tea, but it didn't really matter, seeing as I'd had more than half my cake and the McDonald's lunch and the Smarties. There were still quite a few Smarties left. Just no red ones. Or pink or mauve or blue. They're my favourite colours. But there were plenty of the boring ones to share with the others.

153

When I came out of the Quiet Room I collected my Smarties and the two slices of cake. They'd got a bit squashed as I was saying goodbye to Cam, but Jenny helped me spruce them up a bit and put them on a plate.

I went to find Peter. He was up in his room, sitting on his bed, looking a bit quiet.

'Oh oh,' I said. 'This older couple. They didn't turn up?'

'Oh yes. They did,' said Peter.

'But they were pretty awful, yes? Never you mind, Pete, see what I've got for us? Look, really yummy cake.'

'Thank you, Tracy,' said Peter, and he took his slice absent-mindedly. 'No, they aren't awful, Auntie Vi and Uncle Stanley. They're nice, actually.'

'I bet they didn't take you to McDonald's.'

'No, we went and had fish and chips. My nan and I always used to go and have fish and chips. With bread and butter and a cup of tea.'

'Boring! I had a Big Mac and french fries and a strawberry milkshake, two actually, and then Cam bought me these Smarties and then she bought me this really incredible cake and even put my name on the top. It was my extra special cake and I could have eaten it all up myself but I asked her to save a big slice for

154

you. So I did. And you haven't even started on it yet. Don't you like it? It was meant to be your big treat.'

'Oh, it's lovely, Tracy,' said Peter, munching politely. 'It's ever so good of you. I told Auntie Vi and Uncle Stanley all about you and said that you were my best friend. They want to meet you very much.'

'Well, it's no use them getting interested in me. I'm going to be fostered by Cam, you wait and see.'

'Really? That's wonderful. You see, I think Auntie Vi and Uncle Stanley want to foster me, Tracy. That's what they said. They want to take me almost straight away.'

'So you're zooming off and leaving me in this dump, are you?' I said. 'Terrific!'

'Well. I don't *want* to leave you, Tracy. I told them that. But if you're going to be fostered too . . .'

'Yeah, yeah, well Cam's desperate to have me, but you shouldn't always rush into these things you know, Peter. You should think it over carefully.'

'I know. That's what I've been trying to do,' said Peter. 'Tracy. No matter who fosters me, who fosters you, we can still stay best friends, can't we? And visit each other lots? And write letters?'

'I'll write you letters with my very own

special Mickey Mouse pen. Want to see it?'

'Oh Tracy, you didn't nick it from Cam, did you?'

'Cheek! What do you take me for? She gave it to me, dumbo. I told you she's dotty about me. OK, we'll make a pact. We'll stay best friends no matter what. Here, you're leaving all the icing. Don't you like it?'

'Well, I was saving the best bit till last. But you have it, Tracy. I want you to have it, really.'

It's quite good, sharing a cake with your best friend.

Then I went round the whole Home with the packet of Smarties. I gave one each to everyone. I even gave one to Louise and the new girl. They were upstairs together, trying on the new girl's clothes.

156

Justine was downstairs. At the window. Her dad hadn't turned up. She had a new sticking plaster on her face. She was sniffling.

I looked at her. My heart started going thump thump thump. I went up to her. She turned round, looking all hopeful. She thought I was Louise. But it looks like Louise might have a new best friend now. Louise is like that.

Justine jumped a bit when she saw it was me.

'What do you want, Tracy Beaker?' she mumbled, wiping her eyes.

'I've got something for you, Justine,' I said.

I thought I was going to give her a Smartie. But you'll never guess what I did. I gave her my Mickey Mouse pen.

I must be stark staring bonkers. I hope Cam can get me another one. Next Saturday. When I see her. When she tells me that she's thought it all over and she wants to be my foster mum.

This started like a fairy story. And it's going to finish like one too. Happily Ever After.

The Bed and Breakfast Star

Jacqueline Wilson
Illustrated by Nick Sharratt

CORGI YEARLING BOOKS

For Frances Stokes
(Froggy to her friends)

Do you know what everyone calls me now? *Bed and Breakfast*. That's what all the kids yell after me in the playground. Even the teachers do it. Well, they don't say it to my face. But I've heard them. 'Oh yes, that Elsa. She's one of the bed-and-breakfast children.' Honestly. It sounds like I've got a duvet for a dress, cornflake curls, two fried-egg eyes and a streaky-bacon smile.

I don't look a bit like that. Well, I hope I don't! I'm Elsa.

Do you like my name? I hope you do like it or Elsa'll get upset. Do you get the joke? I made it up myself. I'm always cracking jokes. People don't often laugh though.

I bet you don't know anyone else called Elsa. There was just this lion called Elsa, ages ago. There was a book written about her, and they made a film. They sometimes show it on the television so maybe you've seen it. My mum called me after Elsa the lion. I was a very tiny baby, smaller than all the others in the hospital, but I was born with lots of hair. Really. Most babies are almost bald but I had this long tufty hair and Mum used to brush it so that it stood out all round my head like a lion's mane. I didn't just look like a lion. I sounded like one too. I might have had very tiny little lungs but I had the loudest voice. I bawled day and night and wore all the nurses out, let alone my mum. She says she should have left me yelling in my hospital cot and slipped off out of it without me. She was joking. Mum's jokes aren't always funny though – not like mine.

That was my very first BED.

It's not very comfy-looking, is it? No wonder I bawled.

Here's my second BED.

I used to pretend I was a real lion in a cage. I didn't half roar.

We've still got my old duck cot. We've lost lots of our other things but we've always carted that around with us. I used to turn it into a play-house

or a car

and once it was even
my castle.

But then my sister Pippa was born and I lost a house and a car and a castle and she gained a bed. I gave it a good spring-clean for her and tried to make it as pretty as possible, but I don't think she really appreciated it.

Pippa did a lot more sleeping and a lot less yelling than me. She's not a baby now. She's nearly five. Half my age. She's not half my size though. She's not a little titch like me. She'll catch me up soon if I don't watch out.

I've also got a brother, Hank. Hank the Hunk. He had the duck cot too.

He only fitted it for five minutes. I'm tiny and Pippa is tall but Hank is enormous. He's

not just long, he's very wide too. He's still not much more than a baby but if you pick him up you practically need a crane and if you put him on your lap you get severely squashed. If you stand in his way when he comes crawling by, then you're likely to get steam-rollered.

Pippa and Hank aren't my proper sister and brother. They're halves. That sounds silly, doesn't it. As if they should look like this.

We've all got the same mum. Our mum. But I've got a different dad.

My dad never really lived with Mum and me. He did come and see me sometimes, when I was little. He took me to the zoo to see the real lions. I can remember it vividly though Mum says I was only about two then. I liked seeing those lions. My dad held me up to see them. They roared at me, and I roared back. I think I maybe went on roaring a bit too long and loud. My dad didn't come back after that.

Mum said we didn't care. We were better off without him. Just Mum and me. That was fine. But then Mum met Mack. Mack the Smack. That's not a joke. He really does smack. Especially me.

You're not supposed to smack children. In lots of countries smacking is against the law and if you hit a child you get sent to prison. I wish I lived in one of those countries. Mack smacks a lot. He doesn't smack Pippa properly, he just gives her little taps. And he doesn't smack Hank because even Mack doesn't hit babies. But he doesn't half whack me. Well, he doesn't *always* smack. But he lifts his hand as if he's going to. Or he hisses out of the side of his mouth: 'Are you asking for a good smacking, Elsa?'

What sort of question is that, eh? As if I'd prance up to him and say, 'Hey, Uncle Mack, can I have a socking great smack, please?'

Mum sometimes sticks up for me. But sometimes she says I'm asking for it too. She says I give Mack a lot of cheek. I don't. I just try out a

few jokes on him, that's all. And he doesn't
ever get them. Because he's thick. Thick thick
thick as a brick.

I don't know why my mum had to marry
him. And guess who got to be the bridesmaid
at their wedding! Mum wanted me to wear a
proper long frilly bridesmaid's frock but it
looked ever so silly on me. My hair still sticks
out all over the place like a lion's mane and my
legs are so skinny my socks always wrinkle
and somehow they always get dirty marks all
over them and my shoes go all scuffed at the

toes right from when they're new. The brides-maids' frocks in the shop were all pale pink and pale blue and pale peach and pale lilac. Mum sighed and said I'd get my frock filthy before she'd had time to get up and down the aisle.

So we forgot about the frock and Mum dressed me up in this little black velvet jacket and tartan kilt because Mack is Scottish. I even had a sprig of lucky Scottish heather pinned to my jacket. I felt like I needed a bit of luck.

Mack moved in with Mum and me after the wedding. After I grew out of the duck cot I used to share the big bed with Mum and that was fun because there was always someone to chat to and cuddle.

That was my third BED.

But then Mack got to share the big bed with Mum and I had a little campbed in the living-room. BED number four. And I kept falling out of it every time I turned over at first. But I didn't mind that campbed. I played camping.

But it was really too cramped to play camp. We only had a little flat and Mack took up so much *space*.

There certainly wasn't going to be room for a new baby too. (That was Pippa. She wasn't born then. She was just a pipsqueak in Mum's tummy.) Mum had our name down for a bigger council flat but the waiting list was so long it looked like we'd be waiting for ever.

Then one of Mack's mates up in Scotland offered him a new job up there so he went back up to Scotland and we had to go too. We stayed with Mack's mum. I was scared. I thought she might be like Mack.

But she wasn't big, she was little. She didn't smack, but she wasn't half strict all the same. I wasn't allowed to do anything in her house. I couldn't even play properly. She wouldn't let me get all my toys out at once. She said I had to play with them one at a time.

So I started playing with some of her stuff. She had some lovely things – ornaments and photo albums and musical boxes. I didn't break anything at all but she still went spare.

'You're no allowed to go raking through my things! Away and watch the television like a good wee bairn.'

That's all you were supposed to do in her house. Watch the telly. We watched it all the time.

My Scottish sort-of Gran wasn't so bad though. She did pass the sweets round while we were watching her telly. She called them sweeties.

'Are you wanting a sweetie, hen?' she'd say to me.

And I'd go cluck-cluck-cluck and flap my arms and she'd laugh and say I could be awful comic when I wanted. On Sundays we had special sweeties, a home-made fudge she called tablet. Oh, that tablet. Yum yum YUM.

I could eat tablet all day long. I didn't eat much else at my sort-of Gran's. She said I was a poor wee bairn who needed fattening up but she kept giving me plates of mince and tatties. I don't like mince because it looks as if someone has already chewed it, and I don't like mashed potatoes because I'm always scared there's going to be a lump. So I didn't eat much and she got cross with me and Mum got cross with me and Mack got cross with me.

The worst bit about living there was the bed. BED number five. Only it wasn't my bed, it was my sort-of Gran's. I had to share it with her. There wasn't room in her bedroom for my campbed, you see, and she said she wasn't having it cluttering up her lounge. She liked it when I stopped cluttering up the place too. She was always wanting to whisk me away to bed early. I was generally still awake when she came in. I used to peep when she took her corset off.

She wasn't so little when those corsets were off. She took up a lot of the bed once she was in it. Sometimes I'd end up clutching the edge, hanging on for dear life. And another thing. She snored.

We were meant to be looking for our own place in Scotland but we never found one. Then my sister Pippa got born and Mack fell out with his pal and lost his job. Mum got ever so worried. She didn't get on very well with my sort-of Gran and it got worse after Pippa was born.

So we moved back down South and said we were homeless. Mum got even more worried. She thought we'd be put in a bed-and-breakfast hotel. She said she'd never live it down. (Little did she know. You don't have to live it down. You can live it *up*.)

But we didn't get put in a bed-and-breakfast hotel then. We were offered this flat on a big estate. It was a bit grotty but Mack said he'd fix it up so it would look like a palace. So we moved in. It was a pretty weirdo palace, if you ask me. There was green mould on the walls and creepy-crawlies in the kitchen. Mack tried slapping a bit of paint about but it didn't make much difference. Mum got ever so depressed and Mack got cross. Pippa kept getting coughs and colds and snuffling, because of the damp.

I was OK though. My campbed collapsed once and for all, so I got to have a new bed.

BED number six. It had springs and it made the most wonderful trampoline.

I had a lot of fun in those flats.
I didn't want to leave.

But Mack got this new
job and started to make a
lot of money and he said
he'd buy Mum her
own proper house and
Mum was over
the moon.

Yippee!

I thought it was great once we'd moved into the new house. I liked that house ever so much. It wasn't damp, it was warm and cosy and when Pippa and I got up we could run about in our pyjamas without getting a bit cold. Pippa stopped being a boring old baby and started to play properly. She shared my new bed now but I didn't really mind that much because she liked my stories and she actually laughed at my jokes. We kept getting

the giggles late at night when we were supposed to be asleep, but Mum didn't often get cross and Mack didn't even smack any more. Hank the Hunk got born and he was happy too.

But we didn't live happily ever after.

Mack's job finished. He got another for a bit but it didn't pay nearly so well. And then he lost that one. And he couldn't get another. Mum worked in a supermarket while Mack looked after Pippa and Hank. (*I* can look after myself.)

But Mum's money wouldn't pay all the bills. It wouldn't pay for the lovely new house. So some people came and took nearly all our things away. We had to leave our new house. I cried. So did Pippa and Hank. Mum cried too. Mack didn't cry, but he looked as if he might.

We thought we'd have to go back to the mouldy flat. But they'd put another family in there. There wasn't any room for us.

So guess where we ended up. In a bed-and-breakfast hotel.

Bed and Breakfast

We went to stay at the Royal Hotel. The Royal sounds very grand, doesn't it? And when we were down one end of the street and got our first glimpse of the Royal right at the other end, I thought it looked very grand too. I started to get excited. I'd never stayed in a great big posh hotel before. Maybe we'd all

have our own rooms with satellite telly and people would make our beds and serve us our breakfasts from silver trays. As if we were Royalty staying in the Royal.

But the Royal started to look a bit shabby the nearer we got. We saw it needed painting. We saw one of the windows was broken and patched with cardboard. We saw the big gilt lettering had gone all wobbly and some of it was missing. We were going to be staying in the   oyal H t l.

'O Yal Htl,' I said. It sounded funny. 'O Yal Htl,' I repeated. I thought of a song we sang at school about an old man river who just went rolling along. 'O Yal Htl,' I sang to the same tune.

'Will you just shut it, Elsa?' said Mack the Smack.

'I can't shut, I'm not a door,' I said. 'Hey, when is a door not a door? When it's ajar!'

No-one laughed. Mum looked as if she was about to cry. She was staring up at the Royal, shaking her head.

'No,' she said. 'No, no, no.' She started off quietly enough, but her voice got louder and louder. '*No, no, no!*'

'Come on, it's maybe not that bad,' said Mack, putting his arm round her.

Mum was carrying Hank. He got a bit squashed and started squawking. Pippa's mouth went wobbly and she tried to clutch at Mum too.

'I don't like this place, Mum,' she said. 'We don't have to go and live here, do we?'

'No, we don't, kids. We're not living in a dump like this,' said Mum. She kicked the litter in the driveway. An old Chinese take-away leaked orange liquid all over her suede shoes.

'For heaven's sake,' Mum wept. 'Look at all this muck. There'll be rats. And if it's like this outside, what's it going to be like inside? Cockroaches. Fleas. I'm not taking my kids into a lousy dump like this.'

'So where *are* you going to take them?' said Mack. 'Come on, answer me. Where?'

Hank cried harder. Pippa sniffed and stuck her thumb in her mouth. I fiddled with my hair. Mum pressed her lips tight together, as if she was rubbing in her lipstick. Only she wasn't wearing any make-up at all. Her face was as white as ice-cream. When I tried to take her hand, her fingers were as cold as ice too.

She shook her head. She didn't know how to answer Mack. She didn't have any other place to take us.

'I'm sorry,' said Mack. 'I've failed you, haven't I?' He suddenly didn't seem so big any more. It was as if he was shrinking inside his clothes.

'Oh don't be daft,' said Mum wearily. She joggled Hank and wiped Pippa's nose and tried to pat my hair into place. We all wriggled and protested. 'It's not your fault, Mack.'

'Well, whose fault is it then?' Mack mumbled. 'I've let you down. I can't get work, I can't even provide a proper home for you and the kids.'

'It's not your fault. It's not anybody's fault.

It's just . . . circumstances,' said Mum.

I saw a horrible snooty old gent, Sir Come-
Stances, pointing his fat finger in our direction,
while all his servants snatched our house and
our furniture and our television and our toys. I
was so busy thinking about him that I hardly
noticed Mum marching off into the entrance of
the Royal, Hank on one hip, Pippa hanging on
her arm. Mack shuffled after her, carrying all
our stuff. He turned round when he got to the
revolving door.

'Elsa!' he called irritably. 'Don't just stand
there looking gormless. Come on!'

'What's a gorm, Mack? And how come I've
lost mine?'

'*Elsa!* Are you asking for a good smacking?'

I decided it was time to scuttle after him. I
squashed into the doorway and pushed hard. It
bumped against Mack's leg and he yelled and
stumbled out the other side, cursing. I stayed
revolving round the door by myself. I felt as if I
wanted to go on spinning and spinning. Maybe
if I twirled really fast like a top then there
would be this humming sound and everything
would blur and I'd shoot out into somewhere
else entirely, a warm bright world where
everyone liked me and laughed at my jokes.

I stepped into the grubby foyer of the Royal
Hotel instead. There was a dark carpet on the

floor, red with lots of stains. The thick wallpaper was red too, with a crusty pattern like dried blood. The ceiling was studded with pale polystyrene tiles but several were missing. I wondered if anyone went away wearing one as a hat without noticing.

There was a big counter with a bell. We could see through a glass door behind the counter into an office. A woman was sitting in there, scoffing sweets out of a paper-bag and reading a big fat book. She didn't seem to notice us, even though Hank was crying and Mack was creating a commotion hauling all our cases and plastic bags around the revolving doors and into the hallway.

Mum touched the bell on the counter. It gave a brisk trill. The woman popped another peardrop in her mouth and turned a page of her Jackie Collins. Mum cleared her throat loudly and pinged on the bell. I had a go too. And Pippa. The woman turned her back on us with one swivel of her chair.

'Oi! You in there!' Mack bellowed, thumping his big fist on the counter.

The woman put down her book with a sigh, marking her place with a sweet wrapper. She stretched out her arm and opened the glass door a fraction.

'There's no need to take that tone. Manners don't cost a penny,' she said in a pained voice.

'Well, we did ring the bell,' said Mum. 'You must have heard it.'

'Yes, but it's nothing to do with me. I'm only switchboard. That bell's for management.'

'But there doesn't seem to *be* any management,' said Mum. 'This is ridiculous.'

'If you want to make a complaint you must put it in writing and give it to the Manager.'

'Where is this Manager then?' asked Mack.

'I've no idea. I told you, it's nothing to do with me. I'm only switchboard.' She closed her glass door and stuck her nose back in her book.

'I don't believe this,' said Mum. 'It's a total nightmare.'

I shut my eyes tight, hoping like mad that it really was a nightmare. I badly wanted to be back in bouncy bed number six in the lovely new house. I put my hands over my ears to blot out Hank's bawling and tried hard to dream myself back into that bed. I felt I was very nearly there ... but then Mack's big hand shook my shoulder.

'What are you playing at, Elsa? Stop screwing up your face like that, you look like you're having a fit or something,' said Mack.

I glared and shook my shoulder free. I shuffled away from him, scuffing my trainers on the worn carpet. I saw a door at the end of the hallway. It had a nameplate.

I pushed the door open and peeped round. There was a little man in a brown suit sitting at a desk. A big lady in a fluffy pink jumper was sitting at the desk too. She was perched on the man's lap and they were *kissing*. When they saw me the lady leapt up, going pink in the face to match her jumper. The little man seemed to be catching his breath. No wonder. The lady was *very* big, especially in certain places.

'Excuse me,' I said politely. After all, I'd just been told that manners don't cost a penny.

'Come on now, out of here,' said the big lady, shooing at me as if I was a stray cat. 'And don't hang around the reception area either. I'm sick and tired of you kids turning this hotel into a play-park. You go up to your room, do you hear me?'

'That's right. Go to your room, little girly,' said the man in the brown suit, trying to brush all the bitty pink hairs away.

'But I haven't *got* a room,' I said. 'We've only just come here and we don't know where to go.'

'Well, why didn't you *say*?' said the fluffy pink lady, and she flounced out of the room, beckoning me with one of her long pink fingernails.

Hank was still howling out in the hall. Pippa was whispering and Mum was muttering and Mack was pacing the carpet like a caged animal, looking as if he was ready to bite someone.

'*So* sorry to have kept you waiting,' said the big lady, and she nipped round the corner of the counter and smiled a big pink lipsticky smile. 'On behalf of the management, I'd like to welcome you to the Royal Hotel. I hope your stay with us will be a pleasant one.'

'Well, we're hardly here on holiday,' said Mum, wrestling with Hank. She sat him down on the counter to give her arms a rest. Hank perked up a little. He spotted what looked like a very very big pink bunny rabbit and started crawling rapidly towards it, drooling joyfully.

'Please try to keep your children under control!' said the big lady, swatting nervously at the advancing baby. 'I'll have to process all your particulars.'

This took for ever. Hank howled mournfully, deprived of his cuddle with the giant pink bunny. Mum sighed. Mack tutted and strutted, working himself up into a temper. Pippa started hopping about and holding herself. There was going to be a puddle on the carpet if we didn't watch out.

'Mum, Pippa's needing the toilet,' I hissed.

'Shut *up*, Elsa,' said Pippa, squirming.

Mum cast an experienced eye at Pippa.

'You'd better take her, Elsa,' she said.

The big lady paused whilst sorting through our particulars and pointed the way down the hall and round the corner. I took Pippa's arm and hurried her along. We passed the Manager's office. His door was ajar. Like my joke.

We had a quick peek at him. He was still sitting at his desk. He'd kicked his shoes off and put his feet up. One of his socks had a hole.

His toe stuck through and looked so silly that Pippa and I got the giggles. The Manager heard and looked cross and we scooted quickly down the corridor. We had to dash, anyway, because it was getting a bit dodgy for Pippa to be laughing in her current circumstances.

Things got dodgier still because we seemed to take a wrong turning and blundered around unable to find the toilets. We came across a gang of boys as we rounded a corner. They were busy writing something on the wall with black felt-tip pen.

'Don't ask them, they'll laugh at us,' said Pippa urgently.

They laughed at us anyway, making rude comments about us as we rushed past. You know the sort of things boys shout out.

'They are *rude*,' said Pippa.

They were ruder than Pippa realized. She can't read yet. *I* read what they were writing on the wall.

We hurried on, turned another corner, and suddenly I saw one of those funny little lady outlines stuck up on the door.

I don't know why they design the lady in that weird sticky-out frock. And she hasn't got any arms, poor thing, so she'd have a job using the loo herself, especially when it came to pulling the chain.

I was still busy contemplating this little lady while Pippa charged inside. I heard the door bang shut.

'Did you make it in time, Pippa?' I called.

'Shut *up*,' Pippa called back.

It sounded as if her teeth were gritted. I stepped inside to find out why. There was someone else in the Ladies. A girl about my own age was sitting on the windowsill with her feet propped on the edge of the washbasin. She was reading a book. Well, she had her eyes on the page, but you could tell we were disturbing her a bit.

'Hello,' I said.

She nodded at me, looking a bit nervous.

'I'm Elsa. And that's my sister Pippa sitting in the toilet.'

'Don't keep *telling* everyone!' Pippa shouted from inside.

'Sisters!' I said, raising my eyebrows.

'Brothers are worse,' said the girl. 'I've got three.'

'I've got one too. He's only a baby but he's still awful. I have to look after him sometimes.'

'I have to look after my brothers all of the time. Only I get fed up because they keep pestering me. So sometimes I slip in here for a bit of peace.'

'Good idea. So what's your name, then?'

'Naomi.'

'Hi, Naomi. I'm Elsa.'

'Yes, you said.'

'How long have you been here then?'

'Sitting in the basin?'

'No! In this place. The hotel.'

'About six months.'

'You haven't! Gosh.'

I was too busy thinking to carry on chatting. I'd thought we'd stay in the hotel a week or two at the most. As if we really were on holiday. I hadn't realized we might be stuck here for months and months.

Pippa pulled the chain and came out of the toilet. Naomi swung her skinny legs out of the way so that Pippa could wash her hands. There weren't any towels so I let Pippa wipe her hands on my T-shirt. Naomi settled her feet back again.

I looked at her. I looked at the tap.

'I could give your feet a little paddle,' I said.

'Don't,' said Naomi.

I thought about it.

'No, OK.'

I smiled at her. She smiled back. Things were looking up. I'd only just got here and yet I'd already made a friend.

I took Pippa's damp hand and we set off back down the corridor.

'I like that girl,' said Pippa.

'That's my friend. Naomi.'

'She can be my friend too. I like her hair. All the little plaits. Will you do my hair like that, Elsa?'

'It looks a bit too fiddly. Come on, quick.' We were going past the boys again. They said some more rude things. Really awful things.

'You think you're so clever, but you can't even spell,' I said, snatching the felt-tip. I crossed out the worst word and wrote it correctly.

That showed them. Pippa and I skipped on down the corridor and eventually found our way back to the foyer.

'There you are! I was beginning to think you'd got lost,' said Mum.

The big lady was handing over a key to Mack.

'One room for all five of us?' said Mack.

'It's a family room, with full facilities.'

Mack stared at the number tag.

'Room six-oh-eight?'

'That's right.'

'That doesn't mean we're up on the sixth floor, does it?'

'You got it.'

'But we've got little kids. You can't shove us right up at the top, it's stupid.'

'It's the only room available at the moment. Sorry,' said the big lady, fluffing up her jumper.

'There is a lift?' said Mum.

'Oh yes, there's a lift,' said the big lady. 'Only the kids have been messing around and it's not working at the moment. We're getting it fixed tomorrow. Meanwhile, the stairs are over there.'

It took us a long while and several journeys to get us and all our stuff up those stairs.

But at long last we were all crowded into room 608. Our new home.

Tea at McDonald's

I thought a family room would have room for a family. Something like this:

199

Only room 608 wasn't quite how I'd imagi-
ned. It was a bit cramped to say the least. And
by the time we'd squeezed inside with all our
stuff, we couldn't even breathe without bumping into each other.

'Home sweet home,' said Mum, and she
burst into tears.

'Don't start on the waterworks,' said Mack.
'Come on, hen, it's not as bad as all that.'

'It's worse,' said Mum, trying to swallow her
sobs. It sounded as if she was clucking. Like a
hen. Mack calls her that when he's trying to be

nice. And he sometimes calls Pippa 'Ma Wee Chook', which is probably Scottish for chick. Hank is too big and barging about to be a chick. He's more like a turkey. I don't get called anything. I am not part of Mack's personal farmyard.

I stepped over all our stuff and climbed across a bed or two and made it to the window. It was probably a good thing it had bars, especially with Hank starting to pull himself up. He'd be able to climb soon and he's got so little sense he'd make for the window first thing. But I didn't like the bars all the same. It felt as if we were all in a cage.

It wasn't just us and our family. We could hear the people in room 607 having an argument. And the people in room 609 had their television on so loudly it made our room buzz with the conversation. The people underneath us in room 508 were playing heavy-metal music and the floor bumped up and down with the beat. At least the sixth floor was the top floor, so there was no-one up above us making a racket.

'It's bedlam,' said Mum.

Bedlam is some old prison place where they put mad people, but it made me think of beds. I flopped down on to one of the single beds. It gave a creak and a groan. I didn't bounce a bit on this bed. I just juddered to a halt. Bed number seven was a disappointment.

I tried the other single bed, just in case that was better. It was worse. The mattress sagged right down through the bedsprings. I set them all jangling as I jumped on.

'Elsa! Will you quit that!' Mack yelled.

'I was just trying out my bed, that's all. Sussing out where we're all going to sleep.' I decided to crack a bed joke to cheer us all up. 'Hey, where do baby apes sleep?'

'Give it a rest, Elsa, eh?' Mum sniffed.

'No, listen, it's good this one, really. Where do baby apes sleep? Can't you guess? Baby apes sleep in apricots.' I waited. They didn't even titter. '*Apricots*,' I said clearly, in case they hadn't got it first time round.

'Sh! Keep your voice down. Everyone can hear what you're saying,' said Mum.

'Then why isn't everybody laughing?' I said. 'Look, don't you get it? Baby apes . . .'

'That's *enough*!' Mack thundered. 'Button that lip.'

Honestly!

Then I had to unbutton, because I'd just thought of something.

'What about Hank? There isn't a bed for him,' I said.

We all looked round the room, as if a bed might suddenly appear out of nowhere.

'This will be Hank's little bedroom in here,' said Pippa, opening a cupboard door that stuck right out into the room, taking up even more of the space. It wasn't another bedroom. It was the shower and the loo and the washbasin, all cramped in together.

'We're going to be able to save time, you know. I reckon you could sit on the loo and clean your teeth and stick your feet in the shower all at the same time,' I said. 'Let's have a try, eh?'

'Look, come out of there, Elsa, and stop mucking about,' said Mum. 'This is ridiculous. Where *is* Hank going to sleep?'

'I'll go downstairs and tell them we're needing another bed,' said Mack.

'Yes, but where are we going to put it?' said Mum. 'There's no room to move as it is.'

'Maybe we'll have to take it in turns to move,' I said. 'You and Mack could stand in the shower while Pippa and Hank and I play for a bit, and then you could yell "All change" and we'll cram into the shower and you two could walk round and round the beds for a bit of exercise.'

I thought it an extremely sensible idea but they didn't think so.

'You'll be the one standing in the shower if you don't watch it,' said Mack. 'And the cold water will be on too.' He laughed. That's *his* idea of a joke.

He went all the way downstairs to tackle the big lady about another bed. Mum sat on the edge of the double bed, staring into space. Her eyes were watery again. She didn't notice when Hank got into her handbag and started licking her lipstick as if it was an ice lolly. I grabbed him and hauled him into the tiny shower space to mop him up a bit. The hot water tap in the basin was only lukewarm. I tried the shower to see if that had any hot. I couldn't work out how to switch it on. Pippa squeezed in too to give me a hand. I suddenly found the right knob to turn. I turned it a bit too far actually.

Mack's joke came true. It wasn't very funny. But at least we all got clean. Our clothes had a quick wash too. I dried us as best I could. I thought Mum might get mad but she didn't say a word. She just went on staring, as if she was looking right through the wall into room 607. They were still having their argument. It was getting louder. They were starting to use a lot of rude words.

'Um!' said Pippa, giggling.

Mack came storming back and he was mumbling a lot of rude words too. The hotel management didn't supply beds for children under two.

'Hank will have to go back in his cot,' he said, and he started piecing the bits of the old duck cot together again.

'But it's falling to bits now. And Hank's so big and bouncy. He kept thumping and jumping last time he was in it. He'll smash it up in seconds,' I said.

'And that's not Hank's cot any more. It's my Baby Pillow's bed,' said Pippa indignantly.

'Baby Pillow will have to sleep with you, my wee chook,' said Mack.

'But he won't like that. Baby Pillow will cry and kick me,' said Pippa.

'Well, you'll just have to cry and kick him back,' said Mack, reaching out and giving her a little poke in the tummy. He noticed her T-shirt was a little damp.

'Here, how come you're soaking wet?' said Mack, frowning.

I held my breath. If Pippa told on me I wouldn't half be for it. Yes, for it. And five it and six it too.

But Pippa was a pal. She just mumbled something about splashing herself, so Mack grunted and got on with erecting the duck cot for Hank. I gratefully helped Pippa find Baby Pillow and all his things from one of the black plastic rubbish bags we'd carted from our old house.

My sister Pippa is crackers. Mack was always buying her dolls when he was in work and we were rich. All the different Barbies, My Little Ponies, those big special dolls that walk and talk and wet, but Pippa's only ever wanted Baby Pillow. Baby Pillow got born when Mum had Hank. Pippa started carting this old

206

pillow round with her, talking to it and rocking it as if it were a baby. He's rather a backward baby if he's as old as Hank, because he hasn't started crawling yet. If I'm feeling in a very good mood I help Pippa feed Baby Pillow with one of Hank's old bottles and we change his old nappy and bundle him up into an old nightie and then we tuck him up in the duck cot and tell him to go to sleep. I generally make him cry quite a bit first and Pippa has to keep rocking him and telling him stories.

'We won't be able to play our game if Hank's got to go in the duck cot,' Pippa grumbled.

But when Mack had got the cot standing in the last available spot of space and we tried stuffing Hank into his old baby bed, Hank himself decided this just wasn't on. He howled indignantly and started rocking the bars and cocking his leg up, trying to escape.

'He'll have that over in no time,' said Mack. 'So what are we going to do, eh?'

He looked over at Mum. She was still staring into space. She was acting as if she couldn't hear Mack or even Hank's bawling.

'Mum?' said Pippa, and she clutched Baby Pillow anxiously.

'Hey, Mum,' I said, and I went and shook her shoulder. She wasn't crying any more. This was worse. She didn't even take any notice of me.

'Here,' said Mack, grabbing Hank, hauling him out of the cot and dumping him into Mum's lap.

For a moment Mum kept her arms limply by her side, her face still blank. Hank howled harder, hurt that he was getting ignored. He raised his arms, wanting a hug. He stretched higher, lost his balance, and nearly toppled right off Mum's lap and on to the floor. But just in time Mum's hands grabbed him and pulled him close against her chest.

'Don't cry. I've got you,' said Mum, sighing. She blinked, back in herself again.

'Where's the wee boy going to sleep, then?' Mack asked again.

Mum shrugged.

'He'll have to sleep with one of his sisters, won't he,' she said.

'Not me!' I said quickly.

'Not me either,' said Pippa. 'He wets right out of his nappies.'

Hank went on crying.

'He's hungry,' said Mum. 'We could all do with a drink and a bite to eat. I'm going to go and find this communal kitchen. Here Hank, go to Daddy. And you girls, you get all our stuff unpacked from those bags, right?'

Yes, everything was all right again. Mum rolled up her sleeves and got the cardboard box with our kettle and our pots and pans and some tins of food and went off to find the kitchen. Mack romped on the bed with Hank, and he stopped crying and started chuckling. Pippa said Baby Pillow was still crying though, and she insisted she had to tuck him up in the duck cot and put him to sleep.

So I got lumbered doing most of the unpacking. There were two bags full of Pippa's clothes and Hank's baby stuff. There was an old suitcase stuffed with Mum and Mack's clothes and Mum's hairdryer and her make-up and her precious china crinoline lady. And there was my carrier bag. I don't have that many clothes because I always get them mucked up anyway. I've got T-shirts and shorts for the summer, and jumpers and jeans for the winter, and some knickers and socks and stuff. I've got a

Minnie Mouse hairbrush though it doesn't ever get all the tangles out of my mane of hair. I've got a green marble that I used to pretend was magic. I've got my box of felt-tip pens. Most of the colours have run out and Pippa mucked up some of the points when she was little, but I don't feel like throwing them away yet. Sometimes I colour a ghost picture, pretending the colours in my head. Then there are my joke books. They are a bit torn and tatty

because I thumb through them so often.

I hoped Mum would be ever so pleased with me getting all our stuff sorted out and the room all neat and tidy but she came back so flaming mad she hardly noticed.

'This is ridiculous,' she said, dumping the cardboard box so violently that all the pots and pans played a tune. 'I had to queue up for ages just to get into this crummy little kitchen, and then when some of these other women were finished and I got my chance, I realized that it was all a waste of time anyway. You should see the state of that stove! It's filthy. I'd have to scrub at it for a week before I'd set my saucepans on it. Even the floor's so slimy with grease I nearly slipped and fell. What are we going to do, Mack?'

'You're asking Big Mack, right?' said Mack, throwing Hank up in the air so he shrieked with delight. 'Big Mack says let's go and eat Big Macs at McDonald's.'

Pippa and I shrieked with delight too. Mum didn't look so thrilled.

'And what are we going to live on for the rest of the week, eh?' she said. 'We can't eat out all the time, Mack.'

'Come on now, hen, give it a rest. You just now said we can't eat in. So we'll eat out today. Tomorrow will just have to take care of itself.'

'The sun will come out tooomorrow . . . ' I sang. I maybe don't have a very sweet voice but it is strong.

'Elsa! Keep your voice down!' Mum hissed.

Mack pulled a silly face and covered up his ears, pretending to be deafened.

We sang the Tomorrow song at school. It comes from a musical about a little orphan girl called Annie. Occasionally I think I'd rather like to be Little Orphan Elsa.

Still, I cheered up considerably because McDonald's is one of my all-time favourite places. Mum changed Hank and we all got ready to go out. It was odd using the little loo in the bedroom. Pippa didn't like it with everybody listening so I trekked down the corridor with her to find a proper ladies' toilet. If Mum saw it she'd get flaming mad again. Pippa got even more upset, hopping about agitatedly, so I ended up trailing her down six flights of stairs and down the corridor to the toilet where we met Naomi. I hoped she might still be there, but she'd gone. The boys weren't hanging around any more either. The rude words were still on the wall though.

We'd worked up quite an appetite by the time we'd trudged up the stairs to put on our jumpers and then down all over again with Mum and Mack and Hank. It was a long long walk into the town to find the McDonald's too. Pippa started to lag behind and Mum kept twisting her ankle in her high heels. I started to get a bit tired too, and my toes rubbed up against the edge of my trainers because they're getting too small for me. Mum moaned about being stuck in a dump of a hotel at the back of beyond and said she couldn't walk another step. Mack stopped at a phone box and said he'd call a cab then, and Mum said he was crazy and it was no wonder we'd all ended up in bed and breakfast.

It was starting to sound like a very big row. I was getting scared that we'd maybe end up with no tea at all. But then we got to a bus stop and a bus came along and we all climbed on and we were in the town in no time. At McDonald's.

Mack had his Big Mac. Mum had chicken nuggets. I chose a cheeseburger and Pippa did too because she always copies me. Hank nibbled his own French fries and experienced his very first strawberry milkshake.

It was great. We didn't have a big row. We didn't even have a little one. We sat in the warm, feeling full, and Mack pulled Pippa on

to his lap and Mum put her arm round me, and Hank nodded off in his buggy still clutching a handful of chips.

We looked like an ordinary happy family having a meal out. But we didn't go back to an ordinary happy family house. We had to go back to the Bed-and-Breakfast hotel.

The people in 607 were still arguing. The people in 609 still had their television blaring. The people in 508 were still into heavy-metal music. And it was even more of a squash in room 608.

We all went to bed because there wasn't much else to do. Mum and Mack in the double bed. Pippa and Hank either end of one single bed. Me in the other. Baby Pillow the comfiest of the lot in the duck cot.

Hank wasn't the only one who wet in the night. Pippa did too, so she had to creep in with me. She went back to sleep straightaway, but I didn't. I wriggled around uncomfortably, Pippa's hair tickling my nose and her elbow digging into my chest. I stared up into the dark while Mack snored and Hank snuffled and I wished I could rise out of my crowded bed, right through the roof and up into the starry sky.

Sugar Sandwiches for Breakfast

We've always had different breakfasts. Mum's never really bothered. She just likes a cup of coffee and a ciggie. She says she can't fancy food early in the morning. She cooks for Mack though. He likes great greasy bacon sandwiches and a cup of strong tea with four sugars. I'd like four sugars in my tea but Mum won't let me. It's not fair. She does sometimes let me have a sugar sandwich for my breakfast though, if she's in a very good mood. I say *she* needs to eat a sugar sandwich to sweeten herself up.

Pippa likes sugar sandwiches too, because she always copies me. Hank has a runny boiled egg that certainly runs all over him. His face is

bright yellow by the time he's finished his breakfast, and he always insists on clutching his buttered toast soldiers until he's squeezed them into a soggy pulp. Sometimes I can see why Mum can't face food herself. Mopping up my baby brother would put anyone off their breakfast.

Mum certainly didn't look like she wanted any breakfast our first morning at the Royal. She'd obviously tossed and turned a lot in the night because her hair was all sticking up at the back. Her eyes looked red and sore. I'd heard her crying in the night.

'How about you taking the kids down to breakfast, Mack?' she said pleadingly. 'I don't think I could face it today. I'm feeling ever so queasy.'

'Aw, come on, hen. I can't cope with all three of them on my own. I'm not Mary Piddly Poppins.'

'You don't have to cope with me,' I said indignantly.

'I sometimes wish to God I didn't,' Mack growled.

He's always like that with me. Ready to bite my head off. He's the one who's like a lion, not me.

I wish I could figure out some way of taming him.

'I'll feed Hank for you, Mum, and see that Pippa has a proper breakfast,' I promised kindly.

'Your mum's going to have a proper breakfast herself,' said Mack. 'That's what she needs to make her feel better. A good cooked breakfast. And if we're getting it as part of this lousy bed-and-breakfast deal then we ought to make sure we all eat every last mouthful.'

'All right, I'm coming,' said Mum, slapping a

bit of make-up on her pale face and fiddling with her hair. She took out her mirror from her handbag and winced. 'I look a right sight,' she wailed.

'You look fine to me,' said Mack, giving her powdered cheek a kiss. 'And you'll look even better once you've got a fried egg and a few rashers of bacon inside you.'

'Don't, Mack! You're going to make me throw up,' said Mum.

I'd throw up if Mack started slobbering at me like that.

We trailed down all the stairs to the ground floor, where this breakfast room was supposed to be. Mack started sniffing, his hairy nostrils all aquiver.

'Can't smell any bacon sizzling,' he said.

We soon found out why. There wasn't any bacon for breakfast. There wasn't very much of anything. Just pots of tea and bowls of corn-flakes and slices of bread, very white and very square, like the ceiling tiles in reception. You just went and served yourself and sat at one of the tables.

'No bacon?' said Mack, and he stormed off to the reception desk.

'Hank needs his egg,' said Mum, and she marched off after Mack, Hank balanced on her hip.

Pippa and I sighed and shrugged our shoulders. We straggled off after them.

The big lady was behind the desk. She was wearing a fluffy blue jumper this time. I hoped she'd painted her fingernails blue to match, but she hadn't. Still, Mack was certainly turning the air blue, shouting and swearing because there weren't any cooked breakfasts.

'It's your duty to provide a proper breakfast. They said so down at the Social. I'm going to report you,' Mack thundered.

'We don't have any duty whatsoever, sir. If you don't care to stay at the Royal Hotel then why don't you leave?' said the big lady.

'You know very well we can't leave, because we haven't got anywhere else to go. And it's a disgrace. My kids need a good breakfast – my baby boy needs his protein or he'll get ill,' said Mum.

She spoke as if Hank was on the point of starving right this minute, although she was sagging sideways trying to support her strapping great son. He was reaching longingly for this new blue bunny.

The big lady stepped backwards, away from his sticky clasp.

'We're providing extra milk for all the children at the moment. We normally do provide a full cooked breakfast but unfortunately we are temporarily between breakfast chefs, so in these circumstances we can only offer a continental breakfast. Take it – or leave it.'

We decided to take it.

'Continental breakfast!' said Mum, as we sat at a table in the corner. 'That's coffee in one of them cafetière thingys and croissants, not this sort of rubbish.' She flapped one of the limp slices of bread in the air. 'There's no goodness in this!'

There were little packets of butter and pots of marmalade. And sugar lumps. Lots of sugar lumps.

I got busy crushing and sprinkling. I made myself a splendid sugar sandwich. Pippa tried to make herself one too, but she wasn't much good at crushing the lumps. She tried bashing them hard on the table to make them shatter.

'Pippa! Give over, for goodness sake. Whatever are you doing?' said Mum, spooning cornflakes into Hank.

'It's Elsa's fault. Pippa's just copying her,' said Mack. 'Here, give me that sugar bowl and stop messing around. You'll rot your teeth and just have empty gums by the time you're twelve.'

I covered my teeth with my lips and made little gulpy noises to see what it would be like. I tried sucking at my sandwich to see if I'd still be able to eat without teeth. I swallowed before the lump in my mouth got soft enough, and choked.

'Elsa! Look, do you have to show us all up?' Mum hissed.

'Stop it!' said Mack. 'Otherwise you'll get a good smacking, see?'

I saw. I was trying like anything to stop choking. I got up, coughing and spluttering, and went over to the service hatch to get myself some more milk. There was a big black lady with a baby serving herself. I wondered if she might be Naomi's mum and asked her between coughs.

She said she wasn't, but helpfully banged me on the back. I took a long drink of milk and peered all round the room, hoping to spot Naomi. There were old people and young people and lots of little kids, black people and white people and brown people and yellow people, quiet people and noisy people and absolutely bawling babies. But I couldn't spot Naomi anywhere. Maybe she had her breakfast sitting in the washbasin in the Ladies.

I did spot one of the boys who'd been writing rude words all over the wall. He saw me looking at him and crossed his eyes and stuck out his tongue. I did likewise.

'Elsa!' Mum came and yanked me back to our table. 'Don't you dare make faces like that.'

I pulled another face, because I was getting fed up with everyone picking on me when it wasn't my fault. Then I saw a lovely lady with lots of little plaits come into the breakfast room. She had two little boys with her, and she was carrying a toddler. And there was a girl following on behind, her head in a book.

'NAOMI!' I yelled excitedly, jumping up.

Mack was taking a large gulp of tea at that precise second. Somehow or other the tea sprayed all down his front. He didn't look too happy. I decided to dash over to Naomi pretty sharpish.

'Hi, Naomi. I've been looking out for you. Is this your mum? Are these your brothers?'

I said hello to them all and they smiled and said hello back.

'Is that your dad over there? That man shouting at you,' said Naomi.

'No fear,' I said. 'What are you reading then, eh?'

I had a quick peer. The cover said *Little Women* and there was a picture of four girls in old-fashioned frocks.

'*Little Women*?' I said, thinking it a rather naff title.

'It's a lovely book, one of the classics,' said Naomi's mum proudly. 'My Naomi's always reading it.'

'Boring,' I mumbled, peering at the pages.

'*The Cursed Werewolf seized the young maiden and ripped her to pieces with his huge yellow teeth. . .*'

'There's a werewolf in *Little Women*?' I said, astonished.

'Sh!' said Naomi, giving me a nudge. She turned her back so that her mum couldn't see and quickly lifted the dustjacket off *Little Women*. She had a different book entirely underneath. *The Cursed Werewolf Runs Wild.*

'Ah,' I said. I decided I liked Naomi even more.

I sat down at their table, even though Mack was bellowing fit to bust for me to come back at once OR ELSE. Naomi's little brothers looked utterly angelic above the table, all big eyes

and smiley mouths, but they were conducting a violent kicking match out of sight. One of the kicks landed right on my kneecap. I gave a little scream and both boys looked anxiously at their mum. I didn't tell tales, but I seized hold of several skinny legs and tickled unmercifully. They squirmed and doubled up.

'Boys!' said Naomi's mum. 'Stop messing about.'

She was trying to feed the baby but he kept fidgeting and turning his head away, not wanting his soggy old cornflakes.

'Come on, Nathan,' said Naomi's mum.

Nathan shut his mouth tight and let cornflake mush dribble down his chin.

'How about feeding him like an aeroplane?' I suggested. 'My baby brother Hank likes it when I do that. Here, I'll show you.'

I took the spoon, filled it with flakes, and then let my arm zoom through the air above Nathan's head.

'Here's a loaded jumbo jet coming in to land,' I said and made very loud aeroplane noises.

Nathan opened his mouth in astonishment and I shoved the spoon in quick.

'Unloading bay in operation,' I said, and I unhooked the empty spoon from his gums.

'Come on then, Nathan, gobble gobble, while I go looking for the next aeroplane. Hey, how about a Concorde this time?'

Nathan chewed obediently while I reloaded the spoon and held it at the right Concorde angle. I revved up my sound system.

Unfortunately, my dear non-relative Uncle Mack was revving up his own sound system. After one last bellow he came charging like a bull across the breakfast room.

I landed Concorde, unloaded the new cargo of cornflakes inside Nathan, and tried turning the spoon into a bomber plane with mega-quick, whizz-bang missiles.

Mack certainly exploded. But not in the way I wanted.

'How dare you make this ridiculous noise and bother these poor people,' he roared, yanking me up from the table.

'Oh no, she's been no bother at all,' said Naomi's mum quickly. 'So Elsa's your daughter, is she?'

'No!' I said.

227

'No!' Mack said.

It was about the only thing we ever agreed on.

'Elsa is my stepdaughter,' said Mack. He said the word 'step' as if it was some disgusting swear word. 'I've done my best to bring her up as if she was my own, but she gets right out of hand sometimes.'

I wished I was out of his hand at that precise moment. He was holding me by the shoulders, his fingers digging in hard.

'Well, she's been a very good girl with us, helping me keep my family in order,' said Naomi's mum.

'Yes, she got my baby brother Nathan to eat up all his cornflakes,' said Naomi.

'It's a pity she can't help out with her own brother and sister then,' said Mack. 'Come on, Elsa, your mum needs you.'

He gave a jerk and a pull. I had to go with him or else get my arm torn off. I looked back at Naomi.

'The Cursed Werewolf!' I mouthed, nodding at Mack.

Naomi nodded, grinning at me sympathetically.

I needed sympathy. Mack was in a foul mood.

'What do you think you're doing, rushing

228

around yelling your head off?' he yelled, rushing around.

I could sense it wasn't quite the right time to point out that I was only following my step-daddy's example. He got me sat back at our table and started giving me this right old lecture about learning to do as I was told. Pippa started fidgeting and shifting about on her chair as if she were the one getting the lecture, not me.

'I'm needing to go to the toilet,' she announced.

'Well, off you go then,' said Mack.

'I can't find it by myself,' said Pippa.

'I'll take her,' I said, jumping at the chance.

I clutched Pippa's hand and escaped the Werewolf's copious curses. Some of the boys were back down the corridor, writing more rude words on the walls. An old lady with a hoover rounded a corner and saw what they were up to.

'Here, you clean that off, you little varmints,' she yelled, aiming her vacuum at them.

They laughed and said the words to her.

'Dirty beasts,' said the hoover lady.

She saw us gawping.

'Cover your ears up, girls. And you'd better close your eyes too. These little whatsits are

desecrating this hotel. Blooming desecrating it, that's what they are.' She banged up against the boys with the vacuum, running the suction nozzle up and down the nearest's shell suit.

'Get off, will you! My mum's only just bought me this,' he yelled indignantly.

'I'm just trying to clean you up, laddie. Get some of the dirt off you. Now clear off, the lot of you, or I'll fetch the Manager.'

They straggled away while she held her vacuum aloft in victory. Pippa and I giggled. Mrs Hoover followed us into the Ladies so she could have a quick smoke.

'Dear oh dear, this place will be the death of me,' she said, lighting up. She tucked her ciggies and matches back in her pocket and flexed her legs in her baggy old trousers. 'It used to be a really classy establishment back in the old days. A really nice business hotel. You could get fantastic tips and everyone spoke to you ever so pleasant. Now you just get a mouthful of abuse. They're all scum that stay here now. Absolute scum.'

She said this very fiercely and then blinked a bit at me.

'No offence meant, dearie. You seem very nice little girls, you and your sister.'

'Are we just a bit scummy round the edges then?' I said.

'You what? Oh, give over!' She drew on her cigarette, chuckling.

'What's scum?' said Pippa, emerging from the toilet and going to wash her hands.

'That's scum,' I said, wiping my finger round the edge of the grey basin.

'Now dear, don't shame me. I used to keep this place so clean you could eat your dinner out of one of them basins. But now I just lose heart. And the management's so mean, they keep cutting down the staff. How can I keep all this place spick and span, eh, especially with my legs.' She patted at her trousers and shook

231

her head. Then she had another glance at the basin. 'Look, that's a footprint, isn't it? Dear goodness, would you credit it? They're actually putting their feet in the basins now.'

'I wonder who on earth that could be,' I said, winking at Pippa.

'I know!' said Pippa, not understanding my meaningful wink.

'No you don't,' I said quickly. 'Here, we could help you do a bit of the cleaning if you like, Pippa and me. I'm good at vacuuming. It's fun.'

I wasn't in any hurry to get back to the breakfast room and Mack. I wanted him to cool down a bit first. So Mrs Hoover sat stiffly on the stairs and did a bit of dusting and Pippa pottered about with a dustpan and brush while I switched on the vacuum and sucked up all the dust on the shabby carpet.

I kept imagining Mack was standing right in front of me. I'd charge at him and knock him flying and then get out a really giant suction nozzle. I wouldn't just snag his shell suit, *oh* no. I'd hoover him right out of existence.

I was galloping along the corridor, laughing fit to bust, when the real Mack suddenly came round the corner. He didn't look very cool at all. He looked as if he might very well be at boiling point.

'What the heck are you playing at, Elsa?'

'I'm not playing, I'm helping do the housework.'

'Switch it off! And don't answer me back like that,' Mack said. 'We thought you'd both got lost. You've been gone nearly half an hour. Didn't you realize you'd be worrying your mum? Elsa!'

'I thought you didn't want me to answer you,' I said.

Mack took a step nearer to me, breathing fire.

'Don't be cross with the kiddie, she's been ever such a help,' said Mrs Hoover. 'She's got this carpet up a treat, I'm telling you. And the little one's been sweeping the stairs, haven't you, pet?'

'Yes, well, I'll thank you to mind your own business,' said Mack, snatching Pippa up into his arms. 'You come with Daddy, chook. We've been worried sick, wondering what had happened to you.

Mum's been right up to our room and back, thinking you'd gone up there.'

Mack stomped round the corner, still clutching Pippa, and tripped right over the gang of giggling boys writing more dirty words on the wall.

'Get out of my way, you kids,' Mack thundered.

Pippa peered at the words from her new vantage point. She stared at the worst word of all. She remembered. She said it loudly and clearly.

'What did you say, Pippa?' said Mack, so taken aback he nearly dropped her.

So she said it again. Unmistakably.

'I'm reading, Dad,' she said proudly.

The boys absolutely cracked up at this, sniggering and spluttering.

'I'll wipe the smile off your silly faces!' Mack shouted, practically frothing at the mouth. 'How dare you write mucky words on the wall so that my little girl learns dirt like that?'

They stopped sniggering and started scattering, seeing that Mack meant business. Mack caught hold of one of them, the boy I'd made the face at. He was pulling faces again now, trying to wriggle free.

'It wasn't me that wrote that word, honest!' he yelled. 'It was her.'

He pointed to me. All his pals stopped and pointed to me too.

'Yes, it was that girl.'

'Yes, that one with all the hair.'

'Yeah, that little girl with the loud voice.'

It looked like I was in BIG TROUBLE.

I was.

I tried to explain but Mack wouldn't listen.

He hit. And I hurt.

Sweets for Treats

Mack stayed in a horrible mood all that day. All that *week*. And Mum wasn't much better. She didn't get mad at me and shout. She didn't say very much at all. She did a lot of that sitting on the bed and staring into space. Sometimes Mack could snap her out of it. Sometimes he couldn't.

I hated to see Mum all sad and sulky like that. I tried telling her jokes to cheer her up a bit.

'Hey Mum, what's ten metres tall and green and sits in the corner?'

'Oh Elsa, please. Just leave me be.'

'The Incredible Sulk!'

I fell about. But Mum didn't even smile.

'OK, try this one. Why did the biscuit cry?'

'What biscuit? What are you on about?'

'Any biscuit.'

'Can I have a biscuit, Mum?' said Pippa.

'Look, just listen to the *joke*. Why did the biscuit cry, eh? Because his mother was a wafer so long.'

I paused. Nobody reacted.

'Don't you get it?'

'Just give it a rest, Elsa, please,' Mum said, and she lay back on her bed and buried her head under the pillow.

I stared at Mum worriedly. I so badly wanted her to cheer up.

'Mum? Mum.' I went over to her and shook her arm.

'Leave her be,' said Mack.

I took no notice.

'Mum, what happened to the lady who slept with her head under the pillow?'

Mum groaned.

'When she woke up she found the fairies had taken all her teeth out!'

Mum didn't twitch.

'Elsa, I'm telling you. Leave her alone,' Mack growled.

I tried just one more.

'Are you going to sleep, Mum? Listen, what happened to the lady who dreamed she was eating a huge great marshmallow?'

'Can I have a marshmallow?' said Pippa.

'When she woke up her pillow had disappeared!'

Mum didn't move. But Mack did.

'I'm warning you, Elsa. Just one more of your stupid jokes and you're for it!'

'Dad, can I have some biscuits or some sweets or something? I'm hungry,' Pippa whined.

'OK, OK.' Mack fumbled in his pocket for change. 'Take her down to that shop on the corner, Elsa. Here.'

'What do Eskimos use for money? Ice lolly!'

'I thought I told you. NO MORE JOKES!'

'OK, OK.' I grabbed Pippa and scooted out the room.

'Why are adults boring?' I asked her, as we went down the stairs. 'Because they're groan-ups.'

I roared with laughter. I'm not altogether sure Pippa understood, but she laughed too to keep me company. The big bunny lady in reception put her pointy finger to her lips and went 'Sh! Sh!' at us.

'She sounds like a train,' I said to Pippa. 'Hey, what do you call a train full of toffee?'

'Oh, toffee! Are you buying toffee? I like toffee too.'

'No, Pippa, you're not concentrating. What do you call a train full of toffee? A chew-chew train.'

Pippa blinked up at me blankly. I laughed. She laughed too, but she was just copying me like she always does. I wished she was old enough to appreciate my jokes. I longed to try them all out on Naomi, but she was at school.

That was one of the advantages of going to live at the O Yal Htl. I couldn't go to my old school because it was miles and miles away. No-one had said anything about going to any other school. I certainly wasn't going to bring the subject up.

I took hold of Pippa's hand and we went out of the hotel and down the road to where there was this one shop selling sweets and ciggies and papers and videos – all the things you need.

Some of the boys from the hotel were mucking around at the video stands, whizzing them round too fast and acting out bits from the films. One of them lunged at me with his hands all pointy, pretending to be Freddie from Elm Street.

'Ooooh, I'm so fwightened,' I said, sighing heavily. 'What are you lot doing here, anyway? Are you bunking off from school?'

They shuffled a bit so I was obviously right.

'Don't you tell on us or you'll get it, see,' said another, trying to act dead tough.

'Don't worry. *I* don't tell tales,' I said, looking witheringly at the funny-face boy who had told on me.

He shuffled a bit more, his face going red.

'Yeah, well, I didn't think your dad would get mad at you like that,' he said quickly.

'He's not my dad. He's just my mum's bloke, that's all.'

'Did he hit you? We heard you yelling.'

'You'd yell if he was laying into you.'

'Here. Have this,' said the funny-face boy, and he handed me his big black magic-marker pen, the one I'd used to correct his spelling to write the truly worst word ever.

'Hey, are you giving this to me?' I said.

'Yeah, if you want.'

'You bet I want! My own black felt-tip's run out. Hey, what goes black and white, black and white, black and white?'

'Hmm?' he said, looking blank.

But one of his mates spoilt it.

'A nun rolling down a hill,' he said, grinning. 'That's an *old* joke.'

'OK, OK, what's black and white and goes ha-ha?'

I paused. This time I'd got them.

'The nun that pushed her!'

Funny-face suddenly snorted with laughter. The others all sniggered too. Laughing at my joke! I'd have happily stood there cracking jokes all day but the man behind the counter started to get narked so the boys sloped off while Pippa and I chose our sweets. It took a long time, especially as Pippa kept chopping and changing. Once or twice she changed her mind *after* she'd had a little experimental lick of a liquorice bootlace or a red jelly spider, but the man behind the counter couldn't see down far enough to spot her.

241

We ended up with:

We ate them on the way back to the hotel. We weren't in any hurry to get back. Mack had been so grouchy recently he'd even got mad at Pippa.

I meant to save a chocolate bar for Naomi, and a toffee chew or two for her brothers, but I seemed to get ever so hungry somehow, and by the time Naomi got back from school there were just a few dolly mixtures left (and they were a bit dusty and sticky because Pippa had been 'feeding' them to Baby Pillow half the afternoon).

'Never mind, I'll give them a little wash under the tap,' said Naomi, going into the Ladies.

She and I scrunched up together on the windowsill, feet propped on the basin, and we read the worst bits of her Cursed Werewolf book and got the giggles. My Pippa and her Nicky and Neil and Nathan kept on plaguing us so we filled the other basins with water and hauled them up so they could have a little paddle. They were only meant to dangle their feet. They dangled quite a bit more.

I was scared I'd get into trouble with Mum and Mack for getting Pippa soaked, but luckily Mum didn't notice and Mack had gone out for a takeaway and taken Hank with him. Hank loves to go anywhere with Mack. He's a really weird baby. He thinks his dad is great.

I think Mack is great too. A great big hairy warthog.

Pippa and Nicky and Neil and Nathan weren't the only ones who got soaked when they went paddling in the basins. The floor in the Ladies turned into a sort of sea too. Naomi and I tried to mop it up a bit but we only had loo paper to do it with so we weren't very successful.

Mrs Hoover had to mop it up properly and she wasn't very pleased. I felt bad about it so the next day Pippa and I helped her with her hoovering. I'd got lumbered with Hank as well, but I tried hard to get him to flick a duster. He seemed determined to use it as a cuddle blanket but Mrs Hoover didn't mind.

'Oh, what a little sweetie! Bless him!' she cooed.

'Have you got some sweeties?' Pippa asked hopefully.

'You're just like my little granddaughter, pet. Always on at her Nan for sweeties. Here you are, then.' Mrs Hoover gave us both a fruit drop. Hank had to make do with chewing his duster, because he might swallow the fruit drop whole and choke.

'Yum yum, I've got an orange. I nearly like them best. I like the red bestest of all,' said Pippa hopefully.

I tutted at her but Mrs Hoover tittered.

'You're a greedy little madam,' she said, handing over a raspberry drop too.

'What do you say, Pippa, eh?' I said.

'Thank you ever so much Mrs Hoover.'

'You what?' said Mrs Hoover, because Mrs Hoover wasn't her real name at all, it was just our name for her. Her real name was Mrs Macpherson but I didn't like calling her that because it reminded me too much of my Mack Person. My least favourite person of all time.

He'd given me another smack because Pippa and I were playing hunt the magic marble in our room and I'd hidden it under the rug covering the torn part of the carpet. How was I to know that Mack would burst back from the betting shop and stomp across the rug and skid on the marble and go flying?

I couldn't help laughing. He really did look hilarious. Especially when he landed bonk on his bum.

'I'll teach you not to laugh at me!' he said, scrabbling up.

He did his best.

But I've had the last laugh. I sloped off into the Ladies all by myself and had a little fun with my new black magic-marker pen.

Mega-Feast for Lunch

I soon got into a Royal Hotel routine. I always woke up early. I'd scrunch up in bed with my torch and my joke books and wise up on a few more wisecracks. I'd tell the jokes over and over until I had them off by heart. I'd often roll around laughing myself.

Sometimes I shook the bed so much Pippa woke up wondering if she was in the middle of an earthquake. If I caused earthquakes Pippa was liable to cause her own natural disasters. Floods.

Mum kept getting mad at her and saying she was much too big to be wetting the bed and she didn't let Pippa have anything to drink at teatime but it still didn't make much difference. Pippa cried because she was so thirsty and she *still* wet the bed more often than not.

So another of my little routines was to sneak all Pippa's wet bedclothes down to the laundry room before Mum and Mack woke up. There were only two washing machines and one dryer. You usually couldn't get near them. But early in the morning everyone was either fast asleep or getting the kids ready for school so there was a good chance I could wash the sheets out for my leaky little sister.

The only other people around were some of the Asian ladies in their pretty clothes. They looked like people out of fairy tales instead of ordinary mums in boring old T-shirts and leggings. They sounded as if they were saying strange and secret things too as they

whispered together in their own language. Some of their children could speak good English even though they'd only been over here a few months, but the mums didn't bother. They generally just stuck in a little clump together.

I felt a bit shy of them at first and I think they felt shy with me too. But after a few encounters in the laundry room we started to nod to each other. One time they'd run out of washing powder so I gave them a few sprinkles of ours. The next day they gave me half a packet back *and* a special pink sweet. It was the sweetest sweet I'd ever eaten in my life. It was so sweet it started to get sickly, and when I got back to room 608 I passed it on to Pippa. She enjoyed it hugely for a while but it finally got the better of her too. We rubbed a little on Hank's dummy and it kept him quiet half the morning.

Keeping Hank quiet was a task and a half at the hotel. He'd always been a happy sort of baby, even if he did act like a bit of a thug at times, bashing about with his fat fists and kicking hard with his bootees. But he'd never really whined and whimpered that much. Now he didn't seem to do much else. It was probably because he was so cooped up. He was just getting to the stage when he wanted to crawl around all over the place and explore. But he couldn't really crawl in room 608. It was much too little and crowded.

It was dangerous too. If you took your eye off him for two seconds he'd be doing this

or this

or this.

There was only one way to keep him out of mischief.

He didn't like it one little bit. He wanted to be up and about.

Mum and Mack didn't want to be up and about at all. They just wanted to sleep in. Most days they even stopped bothering to go down to breakfast. So Pippa and Hank and I had our breakfast and then we helped Mrs Hoover and then we played about in the corridor. We set Hank down at one end and charged up to the other end and had a very quick game before he caught up with us.

Hank got so good at crawling he could probably win a gold medal at the Baby Olympics. If we wanted any peace at all we had to change his crawling track into an obstacle race.

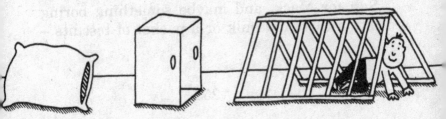

Sometimes we collected several babies and had a proper race. The other brothers and sisters placed bets. That was good. Pippa and I coined it in, because Hank always won.

We got a bit noisy and sometimes Mack would come staggering out into the corridor and tell us all to pipe down. He'd yell if he was in a bad mood but he didn't frighten anyone now. The kids just muttered amongst themselves about pimply bums and brain transplants and cracked up laughing. All the girls had read the jokes in the Ladies toilet downstairs. Even some of the boys had dashed in and out for a dare.

Mack and Mum often didn't get up properly until lunchtime. Lunch was my favourite meal of the day because I could nip along to the shop on the corner and choose it. I had to make sure I bought a packet of ciggies for Mum and the *Sun* for Mack, and maybe something boring like a carton of milk or a packet of biscuits –

but then I could buy crisps and Coke and chocolates and sweets and anything else I fancied with the money left over. Pippa and I always had a Mega-Feast.

SAMPLE WEEK'S MENU OF THE MEGA-FEAST

Monday: Apple juice, Mini Cheddars, Toffee Crisp, Woppa, Spearmint chew

Tuesday: Strawberry Ribena, Californian corn chips, Cadbury's Flake, Buster bar

Wednesday: Lucozade, Chicken Tikka Hula Hoops, Bounty, Flying Saucers

Thursday: Dr Pepper drink, Chipsticks, Galaxy, Sherbert Fountain

Friday: Coke, Salt-and-vinegar crisps, Crunchie, Fizz cola-bottle sweets

Saturday: Strawberry Break Time Milk, Pork scratchings, Picnic, Dollybeads

Sunday: Lilt, Skips (chilli flavour), Fruit-and-nut chocolate, Giant Bootlace

This is all times two, because Pippa always copied me. Hank generally wanted a lick here and a munch there after he'd had his bottle and his baby tins, but there was still heaps left for us.

We sometimes went out in the afternoons. Once we went to the park.

I liked it best of all when Mack went down the betting shop and took Hank along too and Mum and Pippa and me went to the shops. Not the shop on the corner. Not the Kwik-Save or the off-licence or the chip shop down the road. The real shops in the town. Especially the

Flowerfields Shopping Centre. It's this great glass shopping mall with real flowers blossoming in big bouquets all round the entrance, and painted flowers spiralling over the door of each individual shop, and there are lovely ladies wandering round in long dresses who hand you a flower for free.

Mum and Pippa and I could spend hours and hours and hours wandering round the Flowerfields Shopping Centre.

Of course we couldn't ever buy the books or the tapes or the toys or the outfits. But we could go back the next day and the next and read and listen and play and try them on all over again. And then when we had to trail all the way back to the Oyal Htl and we were all tired and we didn't even have the money for the bus, we could still smell our flowers and pretend they were big bouquets.

I made up this story to myself that I was a famous comedienne and I'd just done this amazingly funny routine on stage and everyone had laughed and laughed and then they'd clapped and clapped and begged for an encore and showered me with roses . . .

'Hey, Mum, Pippa, what do you get if you cross a rose with a python?'

'Oh Elsa, please, give it a rest.'

'I don't know what you get – but don't try to smell it!' I laughed. Then I tried again.

'What did one rose say to the other rose?'

'Hello, Rose,' said Pippa. She laughed. 'Hey, I said the joke!'

'Don't you start too,' Mum groaned.

'That's not a joke, Pippa. It's not funny. No, *listen*. What did one rose say to the other rose? It said . . . Hi, Bud. See? *That's* funny.'

'No it's not,' said Mum.

I ignored her.

'All right then. What did the bee say to the flower?'

'Hi, flower?' said Pippa. 'Is that right? Have I said the joke now?'

'No! Pippa, you can't just say any old thing. It's got to be a joke. Now, what did the bee say to the flower? It said, Hello honey.'

'And I'm going to say Goodbye Sweetie if you dare come out with one more of your daft jokes,' said Mum, but she didn't really mean it. She was just joking herself.

Mum could still be a lot of fun, especially going round Flowerfields – but when we got back to room 608 she wilted like the flowers.

We spent the evenings indoors. So did everyone else around us. The people in room 607 had more arguments. The people in room 609 still had their telly blaring. The people underneath in room 508 still played their heavy-metal music. You could feel our room vibrating with the noise.

We tried going downstairs to the television lounge. Well, that was a laugh. There wasn't anywhere to lounge, like a sofa or a comfy armchair. There were just these old vinyl straight-back chairs, the same sort as in the breakfast room, but even older, so you had to play musical chairs finding the ones without the wobbly legs. There wasn't much of a television either. It was supposed to be colour but the switch wouldn't stay stable, so people's faces were gloomy grey for a bit and then suddenly blushed bright scarlet for no reason. There was something wrong with the sound too. It was all blurry and every time anyone talked there was a buzzing sound.

'I'm starting to feel that way myself,' said Mum, putting her hands over her ears.

'Don't throw another moody on me, for goodness sake,' said Mack. 'I can't stick this. I'm going out.'

Mum hunched up even smaller in her chair after he'd gone. I went over to her and tried putting my arm round her. She didn't seem to notice.

'Good riddance to bad rubbish,' I said fiercely.

We both knew where he'd gone. Down the pub. He'd drink all our money and then try to scrounge from some mates. And then he'd come staggering back and be all stupid and snore all night and in the morning he'd have such a sore head he'd snap at the least thing.

I got ten out of ten for an accurate prediction. But by the afternoon he was acting sorry. He'd won a bet down at the betting shop so he took Mum out in the evening while I babysat and then on Sunday morning he got up ever so early. I heard him go out before anyone else was awake. I couldn't help hoping he was maybe doing a runner. But he came back at ten o'clock, staggering again, but this time it was because he was carrying a television.

'I got it for a fiver at a car-boot sale,' he said triumphantly. 'There! Now we don't have to sit in that stupid lounge. We can watch our own telly. Great, eh?'

It wasn't a colour television, just a little old black-and-white portable set. It took ages to retune it when you changed channels, and of course you couldn't get Sky. But it *was* our own television. We could put the sound up so loud you could hardly hear the arguments in 607 and if we tuned into the same programme as the people in 609 it was like we were listening in stereo.

Mum didn't get so droopy now she had the television to watch. She switched on as soon as she woke up and it was still on long after I settled down to sleep. I liked to listen to it as I snuggled under the covers. But sometimes I put my head right down under my duvet and put my hands hard over my ears so that they made their own odd roaring noise and then I switched on this tiny private little television inside my own head. It was much better than the real thing because I could make up all my own programmes.

I was the lady on breakfast television interviewing people in my bedroom

and I was in all the soaps

and I won all the quizzes

and *Gladiators*

and I was in *Blue Peter*

and I was in
lots of films

and best of all I had my very own comedy show
and it was a huge success.

One Slurpy Square of Yorkie Bar

Just when I'd got into this happy little routine at the Royal, Mum went and mucked it all up. She stopped drooping. She started dashing about. She said we weren't going to be stuck in this crummy bed-and-breakfast dump a day longer. She went to the housing department and the social services and the DSS. She armed herself with Hank and Pippa and me, and whenever we were stuck too long in a queue she sent Pippa and me off sniping into enemy territory in quest of a toilet and she primed her Hank hand grenade and set him off howling.

Mum went into battle day after day, but it didn't make any difference to where we lived. We had to stay put because there wasn't anywhere else for us to go. But someone down the Social told Mum about this drop-in centre where the kids could play and you got cheap food, so Mum thought she'd give it a go.

I didn't like the sound of it.

It wasn't that bad actually, just this big room, half of it for the mums and half a crèche for the kids. It was a bit of a crush in the crèche and there was just this one woman going crackers trying to keep all the kids chirpy.

We soon got them sorted out.

But then someone from the Council came and said the centre had to be closed because there wasn't any more money to fund it. Mum started moaning and creating, saying this drop-in centre was practically saving her life because we were stuck in a bed-and-breakfast hotel and it was no place for little kids. The Council Someone got a bit stammery because Mum can get ever so fierce when she feels like it, and he promised to put Hank's name down on the day nursery waiting list.

'Oh, very funny,' said Mum. 'He'll be twenty-one before he gets a blooming place.'

'This little girly here will be old enough for proper school soon,' he said, timidly patting Pippa.

Then he turned to me.

Oh-oh. I should have seen it coming and scarpered.

'Why isn't this girl in school, hmm? Now, I *can* help you here. We'll get her registered at the local school straightaway and she can start on Monday morning.'

Thanks a lot.

It had been the one ultra big bonus of life at the Oyal Htl. NO SCHOOL.

I knew Naomi and Funny-Face and most of the other kids at the hotel had to go. I'd hoped I'd not got noticed. I don't like school. Well, my first school was OK. There was a smiley teacher and we could play with pink dough and we all got to sing these soppy old nursery rhymes. I could sing loudest and longest.

But then we moved up to Scotland and I had to go to a new school and it was all different and I got teased because of the way I talk. Then we moved back down South and lived in the flats and that school was the sort where even the little kids get their heads held down the toilet. That was a pretty grim way of getting your hair washed. I didn't go a bundle on that school. But then the next one, my last school, wasn't so bad. That was when we were living in the lovely house and we were almost an ordinary family and even Mack didn't smack. Well, not so much.

It was a bit depressing though. They gave me all these tests and stuff and I couldn't do a lot of it. They thought I was thick. *I* thought I was thick. I had to go to these extra classes to help me with my reading and my writing and my sums. The other kids laughed at me.

I like it when people laugh at my jokes. But I can't stand it when they laugh at *me*.

But I had this really great remedial teacher, Mr Jamieson, only everyone called him Jamie, even us kids. He was very gentle and he didn't yell at you when you couldn't do something. He worked with me and whenever I learnt the least little thing he smiled and stuck his thumb up and said I was doing really fine. So I

felt fine and I learnt a lot more and then Jamie got me to do some other tests and it turned out I wasn't thick at all. I was INTELLIGENT.

Jamie asked me about all the other schools and he said that it was no wonder I hadn't been able to learn much, because I'd had so many changes. But now I could get stuck in and swoop through all the stuff I didn't know and Jamie said I'd soon end up top of the class, not bottom. So there.

But then Mack lost his job and we lost our house and we ended up in the Oyal Htl, miles and miles and miles away from my old school.

Still, if I had to go to school, that was the one I wanted to go to. So that I could still see Jamie.

'Of course you can't go, Elsa. You'd have to get two buses. And then walk miles. We can't afford the fares. And you'd wear out your trainers in weeks. No, you're to go to this Mayberry School where the other kids go.'

Only they didn't all go, of course. Naomi went. The Asian kids went. One or two others. But Funny-Face and nearly all the boys bunked off every day.

I decided that's what I'd do. I might know I was intelligent, but this school might give me the wrong sort of tests. I could easily end up being thought thick all over again. There was

268

no guarantee at all I'd find another Jamie.

I started hanging around more with Funny-Face and the others. I had to work hard to get them to like me. I had to tell them lots and lots of jokes. They soon got sick of my usual repertoire. Get that fancy word. I'm *not* thick. I know lots and lots of things, though they're not usually the sort of things they like you to know in school. All comedians have to have a repertoire – it's all the jokes in their act. So to impress Funny-Face and his Famous Five followers I had to tell a few rude jokes. Naughty jokes. Blue jokes. Dirty jokes. You know the sort.

The trouble was that Pippa still hung round me most of the time, and she heard some of the jokes too. I told her and told her and told her that she mustn't repeat them, but one time she forgot. She told Mack.

And then guess what. SMACK.

'It wasn't my fault this time,' said Funny-Face afterwards.

'It was my fault,' said Pippa, and she burst into tears.

'You didn't mean to,' I said, giving her a cuddle. 'Here, don't cry, you soppy little thing. It's me he smacked, not you.'

'You don't hardly ever cry,' said Pippa.

'She's tough,' said Funny-Face, and he sounded admiring.

'Yeah, that's me. Tough as old boots,' I said, swaggering.

So on the Monday I was due to start school I set off with Naomi, but the minute we got down the road I veered off with Funny-Face and the Famous Five.

'Hey, Elsa. Why don't you come with me?' Naomi said, looking disappointed. 'I thought we were friends. Why do you want to go off with all the boys?'

'We are friends, Naomi. Course we are. I just don't want to go to this dopey old school, that's all. I'll see you after, same as usual, and we'll play in the toilets and have fun.'

'But it isn't a dopey school, really. And I hoped we'd get to be in the same class. I even swopped desks with this other girl so there'd be a place for you to sit beside me.'

'Oh Naomi,' I said, fidgeting. She was starting to make me feel bad. But I really didn't want to go to school. I didn't even want to be in Naomi's class and sit beside her. Naomi looked like she was really brainy, being a bookworm and all that. I knew I was intelligent, Jamie said so, but I hadn't quite caught up with all the things I'd missed, and maybe it would still look as if I was thick. I didn't want Naomi knowing.

So I went off with Funny-Face and the others. I bunked off with them all day long. It was OK for a while. We couldn't hang about the hotel or risk going round the town because someone would spot us and twig we were bunking off school, but we went to this camp place they'd made on a demolition site. It

wasn't much of a camp, just some corrugated iron shoved together with a blue tarpaulin for a roof. It was pretty crowded when we were all crammed in there knee-to-knee, and there was nothing to sit on, just cold rubbly ground.

'Well, you could make it a bit comfier, couldn't you?' said Funny-Face.

'Yeah, you fix it up for us, Elsa,' said one of his henchboys.

'Why me?' I said indignantly.

'You're a girl, aren't you?'

I snorted. I wasn't going along with that sort of sexist rubbish. They seemed to think they were Peter Pan and the Lost Boys and I was wet little Wendy.

'Catch me doing all your donkey work,' I said. 'Hey, what do you get if you cross a zebra and a donkey? A zeedonk. And what do you get if you cross a pig and a zebra? Striped sausages.' I kept firing jokes at them as the resident entertainer, and so they stopped expecting me to be the chief cook and bottle-washer into the bargain.

They started bullying the littlest boy, a runny-nosed kid not much older than Pippa, getting him to run round the site finding sacks and stuff for us to sit on. He tripped over a brick and cut both his knees and got more runny-nosed than ever, so I mopped him up and told him a few more jokes to make him laugh. It was heavy going. His name was Simon and he certainly seemed a bit simple. But he was a game little kid and so I stuck up for him when the boys were bossing him around and when we were all squatting on our makeshift cushions and Funny-Face started passing round a crumpled packet of fags, I wouldn't let Simon sample a smoke.

'You don't want to mess around with ciggies, my lad, they'll stunt your growth,' I said firmly, and I gave him a toffee chew instead.

I spurned Funny-Face's fags too. I can't stick the smell and they make me go dizzy and I've seen my mum cough-cough-coughing every morning. But even though Simon and I didn't participate in the smoking session it still got so fuggy in the camp my head started reeling. It came as a relief when the blue tarpaulin suddenly got ripped right off and we were exposed by this other dopey gang of boys also bunking off from school. They threw a whole pile of dust and dirt all over us as we sat there gasping, and then ran away screeching with laughter.

So then, of course, Funny-Face and the Famous Five started breathing fire instead of inhaling it, and they went rampaging across the demolition site to wreak their revenge. I rampaged a bit too, but it all seemed a bit ridiculous to me. There was a pathetic sort of war with both gangs throwing stones rather wildly. Simon got over-excited and wouldn't keep down out of range, so he got hit on the head.

It was only a little bump and graze but it frightened him and he started yelling. The boys just stood about jeering at him, though they looked a bit shamefaced. So I rushed over to him going 'Mee-Maa Mee-Maa Mee-Maa' like an ambulance, and then I made a big production of examining him and pretending his whole head had been knocked off and he needed a major operation. Simon was so simple he believed me at first and started crying harder, but when he twigged it was all a joke he started to enjoy being the centre of attention as a major casualty of war.

The war seemed to have petered out anyway, and the rival gang wandered off down the chip shop because it was nearly lunchtime.

That proved to be a major drawback to bunking off. None of us lot had any lunch. We didn't have any spare cash either. As DSS kids we were entitled to a free school lunch but they just issued you with a ticket, not actual dosh you could spend. So as we weren't at school we were stuck. I began to wish I hadn't been so generous with my toffee chew.

One of the boys found half a Yorkie bar he'd forgotten about right at the bottom of his bomber-jacket pocket. The wrapping paper had disintegrated and the chocolate was liberally sprinkled with little fluffy bits and after he'd passed it round for everyone to nibble it was all slurpy with boy-lick too – but it was food, after all, so I ate a square.

I was still starving all afternoon and getting ever so bored with bunking off. I had to keep an eye on the time so as I knew when to go back to the Oyal Htl as if I'd just been let out of afternoon school. When you keep on looking at the time it doesn't half go s-l-o-w-l-y. Half a century seemed to plod past but it was only half an hour.

But e-v-e-n-t-u-a-l-l-y it was time to be making tracks. And then I found out I'd been wasting my time after all. Mum had decided to trot down to the school with Hank and Pippa to see how I'd got on for my first day. Only I wasn't there, obviously, so she went into the school to find me and of course the teacher said I hadn't ever arrived.

Mum was MAAAAAAAAAD.

And then Mack got in on the act and you can guess what he did.

So I stormed off in a huff all by myself.

I sat there and it hurt where Mack had hit me and my tummy rumbled and I felt seriously fed up. But I didn't cry.

And then I heard footsteps. The clacky-stomp of high heels. It was Mum come to find me. I thought at first she might still be mad, but she sat right down beside me, even though she nearly split her leggings, and she put her arms round me. I did cry a bit then.

'I'm sorry, sausage,' she said, nuzzling into my wild lion's mane. 'I know he's too hard on you sometimes.

But it's just that you won't
do as you're told. And you've
got to go to school, Elsa.'

'It's not fair. I don't want
to go to that rotten old
school where I don't know
anyone.'

'You know that nice Naomi. She's your
friend! Oh, come on now, Elsa, you're never
shy. You!' Mum laughed and tweaked my nose.

'The others all bunk off. The boys.'

'I don't care about them. I care about you.
My girl. Now listen. You don't want to go to
school. *I* don't want you to go to school. I'd
much sooner have you round the hotel keeping
the kids quiet for me. I've missed you something chronic today.'

'Really?' I said, cheering up considerably.

'Yes, but *listen*. You've *got* to go to school
because it's the law, see, and if you don't go
they can say I'm not looking after you properly. You know the Social are always on to us
as it is. We don't want to give them any excuse
whatsoever to whip you into Care.'

She'd got me there. So I had to go the next
morning. I set off with all the other kids – and
then when we got to the end of the road,
Funny-Face and the Famous Five all called to
me.

277

'Come on then, Elsa.'

'Come with us, eh?'

'Come to the camp.'

Little Simon even came and held my hand and asked if I'd come and play ambulances with him. His face fell a mile when I had to say no. So I gave him a packet of Polos and showed him how to poke his pointy little tongue through the hole. That cheered him up no end.

'Elsa! Why aren't you coming?' said Funny-Face. 'You chicken or something?'

'Hey, why did the one-eyed chicken cross the road? To get to the Bird's Eye shop.'

'That is a fowl joke,' said Funny-Face.

We both cracked up.

'Come on. You can be good fun . . . for a girl,' said Funny-Face.

'You can be quite perceptive . . .  for a boy,' I said, and I waved to him and walked off with Naomi.

'Is he your boyfriend then?' she said.

'Look, *I'm* the one that's meant to make the jokes,' I said. 'Him!'

'He fancies you all the same,' said Naomi. 'You and him will be slinking off to room one hundred and ten soon.'

'Naomi!' I nudged her and she nudged me back and we both fell about giggling.

The Manager and the bunny lady can't let Room 110 because the damp's got so bad all the wallpaper's peeled off and the Health Inspector's been round. But someone nicked a spare key and some of the big kids pair off, boy and girl, and sneak into the empty room together. They don't seem to mind the damp.

But catch me going anywhere with Funny-Face. Least of all Room 110.

Naomi and I had a laugh about it, like I said, but as I got nearer and nearer the school there suddenly didn't seem anything to laugh at.

'Cheer up, Elsa. It's OK, really it is. Look, tell me a school joke.'

I swallowed. My mouth had suddenly gone dry. For once I didn't really feel in a jokey mood. Still, a comedienne has to be funny no matter what she feels like.

'OK, so there's this geography teacher, right, and he's asking all the kids where all these mountains are, and he says to the little thick one, "Where are the Andes?" and the little thick one blinks a bit and then pipes up, "At the end of my armies." '

My own andies were cold and clenched tight. I felt like the little thick one all right.

Pizza and Porky-Pies

I was right to feel edgy. I didn't like this new school at all.

I didn't get to sit next to Naomi in her class. I was put in the special class, which was a bit humiliating for a start. They said it was just for a little while, to see how things worked out. Hmm. Fine if they did work out. But what if they didn't? Where do you go if you're too thick even for the special class? Do they march you right back to the Infants?

I didn't like my teacher in this strange class I got stuck in.

I wanted a young man teacher like Jamie. Mrs Fisher was old and probably a woman (though she had a moustache above her upper lip).

She also had a hard voice that could rip right through you, though when I first got shoved in her class she stretched her thin lips in a smile and said in ever such sugary, sweetie tones that she was pleased to meet me, and oh what a pretty name Elsa is, and here was my notebook and have this nice sharp pencil, dearie, and why don't you sit at the front where I can see you and write me a little story about yourself.

She was trying to kid on she was really interested in me, but she couldn't fool me. When she took us all out in the playground to have P.E., she got talking to one of the other teachers. The other teacher saw me barging around doing batty things with a bean bag and asked Mrs Fisher who I was. Mrs Fisher didn't even tell her my name. She just said: 'Oh, that's just one of the bed-and-breakfast children.'

I'm not even a she. I'm a That. Some sort of boring blob who doesn't have a name, who doesn't even have a sex.

Elsa the Blob. Hey, I quite like that idea. I could be a great big giant monster Blob and

281

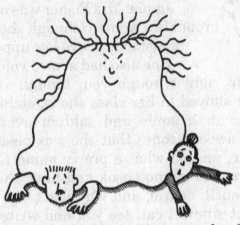

squelch around obliterating people. Mack is still first on my list but Mrs Fisher comes a close second.

I wrote her a little story about myself all right. I wrote that my real name is Elsarina and I'm a child star – actress, singer and comedienne – and I've been in lots of adverts on the telly and done panto and heaps of musicals, and I was actually currently starring in a travelling repertory performance of *Annie* – me playing Annie, of course. And I wrote that my mum and the rest of my family are all in showbiz too, part of the company, and *that's* why we're currently living in a hotel, because we travel around putting on our shows.

I tried to make it sound dead convincing. But when she read it she just gave me one of those smug old smiles.

'This is certainly some story, dear,' she said. 'Rather a *fairy* story, I'm afraid.'

The other kids tittered, though they didn't know what she was on about. She handed me my story back with all my spelling and punctuation mistakes underlined. There seemed to be more red ink on the page than pencil.

But I was not deterred. If I was meant to be thick then some of the kids in the class were as dense as drains, and gurgled into the bargain. So I tried out my Elsarina story on them, and they were all dead impressed, even the big tough guys. I gave them a few quick samples of my comic routine out in the playground and some of them laughed and then I treated them to a rendition of 'The Sun Will Come Out Tomorrow'. I forget what a powerful voice I've got. One or two of them ran for cover, but those that stayed seriously seemed to appreciate my performance.

School didn't seem quite so bad at this stage. I had my little group of fans who happily drank in everything I told them. I got a bit carried away and started elaborating about my mum being this really beautiful actress and yet she could belt out a song and dance up

a storm in this really classy cabaret act . . . and every so often I seemed to step outside myself and hear my own voice and I could see I was tempting fate telling all these lies. Well, they weren't completely lies. Mum *did* use to be beautiful before she met up with Mack and had some more kids so that she lost her lovely figure and gained a few worry lines. She could *still* look beautiful if only she'd bother to slap on some make-up and do her hair properly. She really did use to sing and dance too. She'd sing along to all the records on the radio in a happy husky voice and she'd dance away, wiggling her hips and waggling her fingers. So Mum *could* sing and dance and if only she'd had the right breaks then I'm sure she really could be a star . . .

All the same, I shut up at lunchtime when I met Naomi. It was great to have my own special friend to wander round the playground with. School dinners weren't so bad either. They weren't a patch on my Mega-Feast at home with Pippa, but you were allowed to choose what you wanted, so I had a big plateful of pizza and chips, and I set all our lunch table laughing with a whole load of pizza jokes that aren't fit for publication. Even my silly old chip joke went down well salted.

'Hey, you lot, what are hot, greasy and romantic? Chips that pass in the night!'

The afternoon wasn't so great because we had to divide up into groups to do all this dumb weighing and measuring. I could do that easy-peasy but I didn't have much clue when it came to how you write it all down. I didn't want to admit this so I made a lot of it up, and then of course Mrs Fisher came nosing around and when she saw all my calculations she sighed and scored a line right through them, so it was obvious to everyone I'd got it all wrong. She sat down with me and tried to explain how to do it. I felt stupid in front of all the others and so I couldn't take it in. She had to go through the whole gubbins again, speaking e-v-e-r s-o s-l-o-w-l-y because she obviously thought she had a right moron on her hands. The other kids started to snigger by this stage, so when Mrs Fisher at last left us in peace I had to work hard to regain their respect. I started on about my stage clothes and my mum's stage clothes and my little sister Pippa's stage clothes, and once I'd started on Pippa I couldn't stop, and soon I'd turned her into this adorable little child star with chubby cheeks and a head of curls and though she

hadn't started school yet she could sing and dance like a real little trooper.

I was certainly going a bit over the top here, because even Mack and Mum admit that Pippa is plain. Well, the poor kid can't help it, being lumbered with Mack as a dad. She hasn't got chubby cheeks, she hasn't got curls (Mum did have a go with her curling tongs once when Pippa was going to a party but her hair ended up looking like it had exploded). She isn't even little – she's nearly as big as me though she's half my age – and as for singing and dancing, well, Pippa can't ever remember the words to any song, let alone the tune, and the only sort of dancing she can do is slam-dancing, though she doesn't *mean* to barge straight into you.

But I built her up into such a little Baby Wonder that the kids in my class were drool-ing, and they all wanted to see the show with me and this mega-brilliant little brat and our glamorous movie-star mummy.

'Sorry, folks, we've been sold out for weeks because the show's so popular,' I said breezily, though my heart was beating fit to bust.

That shut them up for a few seconds, but then I started to wonder about going-home time. Mum had caught me out yesterday by trailing round to the school. What if she did it again today? What if she'd just pulled on her oldest old T-shirt and leggings and hadn't bothered to do her hair? All the children would see her for themselves. And even if I could somehow manage to convince them that she was just practising for a forthcoming searingly realistic drama on the telly about a careworn young mother ground down by the system, they'd see Pippa too.

It might help matters if my whole family were present and correct. I could tell them that Mack was all set for a remake of King Kong. He didn't even need to bother with a costume.

287

I shot out of school the moment the bell went. It was a huge great relief to see that Mum wasn't there, though I couldn't help feeling a weeny bit miffed all the same, because she *said* she'd come. She wasn't back at the hotel either. None of them were. I couldn't get into room 608 because I didn't have a key, so I had to mooch about the corridors for ages. Naomi came along but she was a bit narked with me because I hadn't waited for her after school, and she couldn't play with me now anyway because she had to help her mum with her brothers. Then Funny-Face sloped into view, scuffing his trainers and spitting. He was even more narked with me because my mum had stirred things up yesterday and the school had done a check on their registers and sent the truant officer round and now Funny-Face and the Famous Five had to turn up at school tomorrow or *else*.

'Or else you'll all get into trouble and Elsa'll get into trouble for getting you lot into trouble,' I said, pulling a funny face at Funny-Face.

He didn't pull one back. He called me a lot of rude names, even the infamous one he wrote on the wall that I had to correct.

I swept away loftily and pretended I didn't care. But I felt a bit friendless by now. And I was starting to get dead worried that I might be familyless too.

Why had they all pushed off without telling me where they were going? What if they'd finally got fed up with me and packed up and scarpered? I knew Mack didn't want me. He'd go like a shot and he'd take Pippa and Hank because they were his kids and he cared about them. But Mum wouldn't walk out on me, would she? Although only this morning, when the drains all went wrong and someone else's dirty water came bubbling up in our basin, she burst into tears and said she couldn't stick this rotten dump a day longer. So maybe . . . maybe she had gone too.

The ceiling suddenly seemed a long long way off. I felt I was getting smaller and smaller until I wasn't much more than a squeak. I hunched up on the floor with my head on my knees and held on tight in case I disappeared altogether.

'Elsa? What on earth are you doing? What's up, eh?' said Mum, coming down the corridor.

Yes, it was Mum, and I was so very pleased to see her even though she sounded cross. And I was very pleased to see Pippa even though she was all sniffly with her nose running. And I was very pleased to see Hank even though he was howling his head off and needing his nappy changed. And I was . . . No. I wasn't very pleased to see Mack. I wouldn't ever go *that* far.

'Where have you *been*? I've been back from school ages and ages!'

'Yeah, well, I'm sorry, love, but it's not our fault. We had a right ding-dong with that useless Manager this morning because we're all going to end up getting typhoid or cholera stuck in this poxy dump, and the tight-fisted pig won't even send for a plumber to fix things, would you believe! Anyway, he said we could clear off if we didn't like it here, and so I said we were doing our best to do just that, but we didn't have any place to go, so *then* we went down the Housing Office, all of us, and would you believe they kept us waiting *all* day. They weren't even going to see us at all because we didn't have some stupid appointment, but we sat it out and I knew you'd be waiting, pet, but I couldn't do anything, could I?'

'So what happened, Mum? Are we getting a house?'

'Are we heck,' said Mum. 'They just mumbled on about priority families and exceptional circumstances and said even if this dump was affecting our health we'd have to get some really bad complaint and it would all have to be written up in medical reports and even then, if we were all at death's door, they couldn't blooming well guarantee us a house or even a mouldy old flat like we used to have.'

'So I asked what *would* guarantee us a house – did one of you kids have to snuff it altogether, is that it?' Mack said. 'It's getting dangerously close too. Look at little Pippa, all sniffles. She can't get rid of that cold, and as for the baby, well, I don't like the sound of his chest at all.'

Mack sighed over Hank, who was still exercising his magnificent lungs. They certainly sounded in full working order.

'Yeah, Mack started to get really stroppy. Well, I did too, especially when they said they couldn't even guarantee us a proper set of rooms here like we're entitled to, instead of us having to squash up like sardines. They said there was nothing further they could do at this moment in time, and threatened to set the police on to us unless we left the office.'

Mum sighed theatrically, the back of her hand to her forehead. She mightn't be a proper actress but it certainly sounded as if she'd been giving a good performance down at the Housing Office. She threatened to go back again tomorrow, wondering if she could get us rehoused by sheer persistence.

'Yes, good thinking, Mum,' I said, encouraging her so she wouldn't come to collect me from school and crack my credibility.

Only I needn't have bothered. Someone else started telling the wrong sort of tales the very next day. Someone with a funny face. And a great big mouth.

Funny-Face got shoved in the special class too. Right next to me, at the front, under the Fisher's pop eyes. This reminded me of 101 Popeye the Sailorman jokes – *you* know – and I swopped some of them with Funny-Face and we both got terrible snorty giggles, and Mrs Fisher's eyes popped so much they almost rolled down her cheeks, and her mouth went so tight her lips disappeared.

'I'm glad you two are finding school so amusing,' she said, dead sarcastic. 'Perhaps you'd like to share your little jokes with me, hmm?'

Perhaps not. If she heard some of the wilder Popeye jokes she'd go off pop herself.

So Funny-Face and I were getting on famously until playtime. And then one of the kids in the class asked if Funny-Face performed too.

'You what?' said Funny-Face.

'Are you a child star like Elsarina and Pipette?' They elaborated on the famous fictional talents of me and my family, and Funny-Face fell about, thinking this was just another joke, a wind-up on my part.

'You lot aren't half loopy,' said Funny-Face. 'How come you've fallen for all this rubbish? Elsa isn't a famous star! She's just a bed-and-breakfast kid, like me. And cripes, you should see her mum and her dopey little sister – stars!'

That was enough. Funny-Face saw stars then. Because I punched him right in the nose.

All the children started shouting 'Fight! Fight! Fight!' I was all set to have a proper fight even though I'm generally gentle, and Funny-Face was bewildered but wanted a fight too because I'd made his nose bleed. But as soon as we'd squared up to each other Mrs Fisher came flying forth and she seized Funny-Face in one hand and me in the other. She shook us both very vigorously indeed, practically

clonking our heads together, and told us we were very rough, naughty children and we had to learn not to be violent in school.

Then, as she stalked off, she said just one word. Well, she muttered it, but I heard. And Funny-Face did too. She said, *'Typical.'* She meant we were typical bed-and-breakfast kids indulging in typical disruptive behaviour. And I suddenly felt sick, as if I needed my bed and might well throw up my breakfast.

Funny-Face didn't look too clever either. He wiped the smear of blood from his nose and pulled a hideous face at Mrs Fisher's back, crossing his eyes and waggling his tongue.

I giggled feebly.

'Why did the teacher have crossed eyes, eh? Because she couldn't control her pupils.'

It was one of my least funny jokes but Funny-Face guffawed politely.

'Well, she's not going to control us, is she, Elsa?'

'You bet she's not.' His nose was still bleeding. I felt up my sleeve for a crumpled tissue. 'Here,' I said, dabbing at him.

'Leave off! You're acting like my mum,' said Funny-Face.

'Sorry I socked you one,' I said.

'Yeah, well, if that old trout hadn't come along I'd have flattened you, see. Just as well for you. Though you can hit quite hard – for a girl.'

'If you start that I'll hit you even harder,' I said, but I gave his nose another careful wipe. 'We're still mates, aren't we?'

'Course we are. Though why did you have to attack me like that, eh?'

'Because of what you said about my mum and my sister.'

'But you were the one telling porky-pies, not me! Why did you spin all those stupid stories about them? I mean, it's daft. As if you lot could ever be in showbiz.'

'We could, you know,' I said fiercely. 'Well, maybe not my mum. Or Pippa. But *I'm* going

296

to be some day. I'll be famous, just you wait and see. I'll be a comedienne – that's a lady who tells jokes – and I'll have my own show and I'll get to be on the telly, you'll see, maybe sooner than you think.'

It was sooner than I thought, too. Because when Funny-Face and I went home from school that day there was a camera crew filming in the foyer of the Royal Hotel!

Television
and no
Tea

'What on earth's going on?' said Funny-Face. 'Hey, is this for telly? Are we going to be on the telly?'

He pulled a grotesque funny face for the camera, waving both his arms.

I sighed scornfully. I wasn't going to behave like some idiotic amateur. I eyed up all the people and spotted the man in the tightest jeans and the leather jacket. That one just had to be the director. I walked right up to him, smiling.

'Hello, I'm Elsa, I live here and I'm going to be a comedienne when I grow up. In fact, I've got my whole comedy act worked out right now. Would you like to listen?'

The director blinked rapidly behind his trendy glasses, but he seemed interested.

'You live here, do you, Elsa? Great, well, we're doing a programme called *Children in Crisis*, OK? Shall we do a little interview with you and your friend, eh? You can tell us all about how awful it is to have to stay in a bed-and-breakfast hotel, right?'

'Wrong, wrong, wrong!' said the bunny lady receptionist, rushing out from behind her desk. Even the telephonist lady had chucked her Jackie Collins and was peering out from behind her glass door, all agog.

299

'Go and get the Manager, quick,' the bunny lady commanded, shooing the telephonist lady up the corridor. 'Now listen to me, you television people. You're trespassing. Get out of this hotel right this minute or I'll call the police and have you evicted.'

'I can tell any joke you like. We'll have a police joke, OK? What did the policeman say to the three-headed man? Hello hello hello. Where does the policeman live? Nine nine nine Let's be Avenue. What's the police dog's telephone number? Canine canine canine.'

'Very funny, dear,' said the director, though he didn't laugh. 'Now, once we get the camera rolling I want you to say a bit about the crowded room you live in and how damp it is and maybe there are nasty bugs in the bath, yeah?'

'How dare you! This is a scrupulously clean establishment, there are no bugs here, no infestations of any kind!' the bunny lady screeched, so cross that the fluff on her jumper quivered.

'Bugs, OK, I'll tell you an insect joke, right? You've got this fly and this flea, yes, and when they fly past each other what time is it? Fly past flea.' I laughed to show that this was the punchline.

'Mmm, well. Simmer down now, sweetie, we

want you looking really sad for the camera. And you, sonnie, do you think you could stop pulling those faces for five seconds?'

'OK, I can look sad, it's all part of a comedienne's repertoire. Look, is this sad enough?'

'Well, you needn't go to extremes. Cheer up just a bit.'

'Hey, I've thought of another insect joke. There were these two little flies running like mad over a cornflake packet – and do you know why? Because it said, "Tear along dotted line".'

I laughed, but that made me cheer up a bit too much. And then the Manager came charging up and started shouting and swearing at the television people and they tried to film him and he put his hand over the camera and I started to get the feeling I might have lost my big chance to make it on to the television.

'Phone the police this minute!' the Manager commanded.

'I know some more police jokes,' I said, but no-one was listening.

'Who put you up to this? Who invited you in, eh? Has one of the residents been complaining? Which one? You tell me. If they don't like it here they can get out,' the Manager shouted, making wild gestures. He nearly clipped me on the head and I ducked. 'It was your mum and dad, wasn't it, little girl!'

'That man's not my dad.'

'The big Scottish bloke, he was throwing his weight around and moaning about his basin.'

'What animal do you find in a toilet? A wash-hand bison,' I said, but I seemed to have lost my audience.

The police arrived and there was a big argy-bargy which ended in the camera crew having to squeeze all their stuff back round the revolving door, while the Manager continued to rant and rave to me, saying it was all my family's fault and we'd better start packing our bags right this minute.

I began to feel very much like a Child in Crisis. I whizzed out after the camera crew, desperate for one last chance to get on the telly.

'Hey, don't go, don't pack up!' I yelled, as I saw them heaving their gear into a van. 'Look, couldn't we do an interview in front of the hotel, eh? I'll be ever so sad – I could even try to cry if you like. Look, I can make my face crumple up – or I tell you what, I'll go and get my little sister and brother from our room, they're great at crying—'

'Sorry, sweetie, but I think this is a waste of time,' said the director. 'I don't need this sort of hassle. And besides, you're a great little sport but you're not the sort of kid I'm looking for. I need someone . . . ' He waved his hand in the air, unable to express exactly what he wanted. Then he stopped and stood still.

'Someone like that little kid there!' he said, snapping his fingers.

I looked for this favoured little kid. And do you know who it was? Naomi, mooching along the road, trailing a brother in either hand, looking all fed up and forlorn because I'd rushed off with Funny-Face instead of waiting for her.

'Hey, sweetie, over here!' The director waved at her frantically. 'Where did you spring from, hmm? You don't live in the bed-and-breakfast hotel by any chance?'

Naomi nodded nervously, clutching her little brothers tight.

'Great!' He threw back his head and addressed the clouds. 'A gift!'

'We don't want any gifts. We don't take stuff from strangers,' said Naomi, and she started trying to hustle her brothers away. She hustled a little too abruptly, and Neil tripped and started crying.

'Hey, shut up, little squirt,' said Funny-Face. 'You're going to be on the telly. Can I still be on it too, mister?'

'And me?' I said urgently.

'Well, you can maybe sort of wander in the background,' said the director. 'But no clowning. No funny faces. And absolutely *no* jokes.'

I didn't actually feel like cracking any jokes right that minute. Naomi was going to be the star of the show. Not me, even though I'd been perfecting my routine and practising on everyone all this time. Naomi, who couldn't crack a joke to save her life, little meek and mousey Naomi!

OK, I thought. Maybe just *one* joke to try to cheer myself up. So I whispered all to myself,

'What do you get if you cross an elephant with a mouse? Socking great holes in the skirting board!' I couldn't help laughing. You can't really do that quietly. The director glared in my direction. 'Dear goodness, you dippy kids! I don't want merriment, I don't want laughter, I don't want JOKES.'

'OK, OK, no jokes,' I said, and I pinched my lips together with my fingers so he could see I was serious. Only it was such a pity. The mouse and elephant joke had triggered off a whole herd of elephant jokes inside my head, and they were trumpeting tremendously.

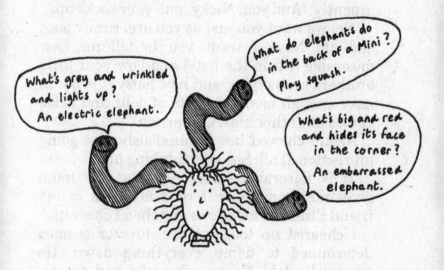

What's grey and wrinkled and lights up?
An electric elephant.

What do elephants do in the back of a Mini?
Play squash.

What's big and red and hides its face in the corner?
An embarrassed elephant.

'Well *I* can't tell jokes,' said Naomi truthfully. 'I can't dance or sing or anything. So you'd really better pick Elsa.'

'Oh Naomi,' I said, immensely touched. 'You can't do all the showy things, but you're ever so brainy. You could get to be on one of the quiz shows, eh?'

'Never mind quiz shows. This little girl's perfect for *Children in Crisis.* Now just stand here, sweetie – little brothers too, that's it, and I'll ask you a few questions while the camera rolls, right?'

'No, wait! Neil, come and get your nose wiped and stop that silly sniffling,' Naomi said urgently. 'And you, Nicky, pull your socks up.'

'No, we want you just as you are, runny nose and all! Now, I want you to tell me how miserable it is in the hotel and how your little brothers keep crying and how lousy it is not to have enough money for lots of dolls and video games like other kids. OK, action!'

Naomi chewed her lip anxiously, not going into action at all. She was thinking hard.

'It *is* miserable sometimes. But my mum gives me a cuddle or I read my book or my friend Elsa tells me a joke and then I cheer up.'

I cheered up too, but the director seemed determined to damp everything down. He practically told Naomi what she had to say.

The first time she had a go she came out all weird and wooden, and she kept looking up at the director anxiously and hissing, 'Is that right? Have I remembered it?'

'No, sweetie, don't keep saying that. Just act natural, for pity's sake,' said the director, practically tearing his hair.

The bunny lady receptionist came clopping out into the street in her high heels, wagging her pointed nails at the television crew.

'Now look! You're harassing our tenants. We'll call the police again. The Manager's on the phone right this minute. And as for you kids, I'm warning you. We don't have to house you, you know. If you've got any complaints then you can push off somewhere else.'

She clip-clopped back into the hotel. Naomi stared after her worriedly, her eyes filling with tears.

'Does she mean that? She wouldn't really throw us out, would she?' Naomi whispered. 'We haven't got anywhere else to go. And it's so unfair, because we've put up with ever such a lot – we've even had those horrible bugs, cockroaches, squiggling all over the floor. One even got in the toe of our baby Nathan's bootee, and yet the Manager wouldn't even send for the pest-control people. He said it was our fault because we were dirty! And my mum cried when he said that because we're as clean as we can be – we bath every day even when there isn't any hot water, and my mum keeps the room spotless, and that's not easy with the four of us kids. I don't know what we're going to do, because we've been waiting six months and we still can't get a flat and if we get turned out the hotel then us kids will have to go into Care and we've got to stay with our mum.'

'We want our mum,' said Nicky.

'Mum! Mum!' wailed Neil.

'Perfect!' said the director. The cameras had been rolling for all of Naomi's outburst. 'Absolutely great, sweetie. Lovely emotive stuff. Right folks, I think we can hit the road now.'

'But what about us?' said Naomi, wiping her eyes. 'Are we going to get thrown out?'

'Mmm? Oh, I shouldn't think so,' he said vaguely.

He'd turned his back on us. He didn't know. He didn't even care. He just wanted to make a good television programme.

I put my arm round Naomi.

'We'll be OK,' I said, giving her a hug. 'Don't take any notice of him. He's just been using us. Still, it looks like you really will be on the telly after all, Naomi.'

Naomi didn't seem very thrilled about the idea. She still worried and worried that her family might get thrown out.

'Look, they've threatened us too. That Manager thinks it's all my mum and Mack's fault. We'll all be thrown out together. We'll have to set up a little camp. It's OK, Naomi. Don't get in such a state.'

I tried to cheer her up, but it wasn't easy.

'I wish you hadn't got us all involved with those telly people,' Naomi said, sighing.

That's what Mum and Mack were saying too in room 608. Only they were saying it a lot more angrily. I could hear them yelling from right down the corridor.

'Oh-oh,' I said.

309

'It's all your fault, you stupid Scottish git!' Mum was screaming. 'You shouldn't have phoned them. Now that Manager will make our lives a misery.'

'It's a flaming misery as it is. It couldn't be worse. I was simply trying to help, so stop giving me all this hassle, woman.'

I slunk into the room. Pippa was crouched in the duck cot, clutching Baby Pillow. Hank was grizzling in bed, needing his nappy changed. I mopped them up and crept off with them. I don't think Mum and Mack even noticed.

It was getting near teatime and there were lots of cooking smells coming from the kitchen. Mum still said it was a filthy hole and we couldn't cook in there or we'd go down with a terrible disease. I was starting to get so starving hungry I was willing to risk the terrible disease, but we didn't have anything to cook.

Naomi's mum was stirring a very interesting bean stew that smelt ever so rich and tasty. She had baby Nathan on her hip, and he was smacking his lips in happy anticipation.

Naomi told her mum all about the television people and the Manager's threats, but Naomi's mum didn't get mad at all. She just went on stirring her stew.

'We'll be fine, little old lady,' she said to Naomi. 'You're such a worry-guts. Here, tea's just about ready. Have you got the plates set out in our room?'

She saw Pippa and Hank and me looking at her hungrily.

'Do you kids want to come and join us for tea?' she said cheerily.

We wanted to extremely badly, but there didn't look that much of a stew and it seemed a bit mean to eat their food so I said we'd be having our own tea in a minute.

But when I did a quick sortie back to room 608 the row was getting louder and fiercer and I knew there was no point disturbing them. So Pippa and Hank and I hung around the kitchen some more. Simple Simon's mum came along and she cooked a whole load of chips in the greasy old chip-pan – so many that they almost came bubbling over the top. They smelt so good and she had such a lot that I decided we'd have a few if we got offered. Only we didn't.

Simon's mum is very fierce.

'What are you kids staring at?' she said

sharply. 'Clear off out of it. Go and get your own tea.'

But that was easier said than done. The row was still roaring. So we sat outside the room, our tummys rumbling. Mack came storming out eventually. He tripped right over me actually. I felt like calling him a Great Scottish Git too, but I sensed it wasn't quite the moment. I knew where he was going. Down the pub. And he wouldn't be back for ages.

At least that meant we could get in our room. But Mum didn't seem up to considering something ordinary like tea. She was in bed crying and when I tried to talk to her she pulled the covers up over her head. She went on crying for a bit and then she went to sleep.

I felt really funny for about five minutes. Not funny ha-ha. Funny peculiar and horrible. It hadn't been a good day. I wasn't going to be on television. I didn't have any tea. I felt like getting into my own bed and pulling the covers up and having a good cry.

But Pippa and Hank were looking up at me and I couldn't let them down. I switched on the telly and said they could stay up as long as they liked because Mum was asleep and Mack was out. And I hunted round the room for food and found some stale sliced bread and a pot of raspberry jam.

'We're going to have a really special tea, you'll see,' I said, scrabbling through Mum's handbag for her nail scissors. I got snipping and scraping and made us ultra-special jam sandwiches.

I made a clown jam sandwich for Hank.

I made a teddy jam sandwich for Pippa and Baby Pillow.

And I made a great red movie-star-lip jam sandwich for me,

and the jammy lips kissed me for being such a good girl.

I woke up early and read my joke books in bed . . .

Why are tall people lazier than short people? Because they're longer in bed, ha ha!

. . . and then Pippa woke up for a cuddle and Hank woke up for a bottle and soon it was time to get up.

Mum didn't wake up. Mack didn't wake up either. He was snoring like a warthog with catarrh.

So I had to speak up to make myself heard. Mum stirred at last.

'Will you stop that shouting, Elsa!'

'I'm *not* shouting,' I said, wounded. 'I'm simply speaking up a little because that Scottish git is snoring fit to bust.'

Mum stirred more vigorously.

'Don't you dare call Mack names like that, you cheeky little whatsit!'

'But that's what *you* called him just last night.'

We started to have a little argument. I might have got a bit heated. Suddenly the warthog stopped snoring. It reared up in the bed, a horrible sight.

'If you don't stop that shouting and screaming right this minute, Elsa, I'll give you such a smacking you'll never dare say another word.'

He glared at me with his bleary eyes and then slowly subsided back under the covers. Hank gave a worried hiccup. Pippa started sucking her fingers. I blinked hard at the bulk in the bed. I opened my mouth, but Pippa shook her head and clutched me with her dribbly little hands. I gave her a hug to show her it was OK. I wasn't going to speak. Mack might be an idle lout but he doesn't make idle threats. He always follows them through.

I waggled my tongue very impressively at

the bed instead. Mum still had her eyes open but she didn't tell me off. When I went to take Pippa and Hank downstairs for breakfast she sat up in bed and held her arms out to me.

'I'm sorry, love,' she whispered. 'I didn't mean to get you into trouble. You're a good girl really, I know you are. I don't know what I'd do without you.'

I cheered up a bit then, but when we went down to breakfast the bunny lady said loudly to the switchboard lady: 'Oh-oh, there's one of the little trouble-makers.' She pointed at me

with a lilac fingernail to match a new purple fluffy jumper. 'The Manager wants to see your dad in his office,' she announced.

'He's not my dad,' I said and walked straight past, Hank on my hip, Pippa hanging on my hand.

'Mack is my dad,' Pippa whispered. 'Is he going to get into trouble, Elsa?'

'I don't know,' I said uncomfortably. Maybe we were all in trouble. Maybe we really were going to get chucked out.

We went to sit with Naomi and her family at breakfast. They were looking dead gloomy too. Naomi's mum didn't smile at me the way she usually did.

'I'll tell you a really good joke about cornflakes,' I said.

'No jokes, Elsa,' she said, sighing.

'OK, I'll tell you this cornflake joke tomorrow. It's a cereal,' I said. I roared with laughter. It wasn't *that* funny, but I wanted to lighten the atmosphere.

Naomi's mum stayed resolutely gloomy. Naomi chewed her lip anxiously. Even Nicky and Neil couldn't crack a smile.

'What's up, eh?' I said, starting to feed baby Nathan, playing the aeroplane game.

He at least seemed happy enough to play, but Naomi's mum caught hold of my arm and took away my spoon.

'No, leave him be. Leave all my family be. Haven't you done enough?'

'Oh, Mum,' said Naomi. 'It isn't Elsa's fault.'

'She was the one who talked you into that television interview,' said Naomi's mum. 'And now the Manager says we'll have to go.'

'Well, he says we've got to go too. But he doesn't mean it. He just wants to scare us,' I said. I tried to sound reassuring but I was getting scared too. 'Look, I'll go and see the Manager. I'll tell him it was all down to me if you like. Then at least you'll be OK.'

So after we'd had breakfast I lumped Hank along to the Manager's office, Pippa trailing behind us. I didn't have a hand free to knock so we just went barging straight into his office. The Manager wasn't on his own. He wasn't having a little cuddle with the bunny lady. He was with Mrs Hoover, and he didn't look at all cuddly. He was telling Mrs Hoover off, wagging his finger at her.

'What's the matter?' I said. 'Why is he being nasty to you, Mrs Hoover?'

'You! Out of my office this instant,' said the Manager. 'It's your mum and dad I want to see, not you lot.'

'I keep telling you, I haven't *got* a dad. That Scottish bloke is nothing to do with me,' I insisted.

'Oh yes! Thank you for reminding me. Yes, my receptionist informs me that there's more disgusting graffiti about a Scots person inside the ladies' downstairs cloakroom,' said the Manager, still wag-wag-wagging that finger at poor Mrs Hoover.

'She didn't do that! I know for a fact that Mrs Hoover didn't write all that stuff on the walls,' I said quickly, my heart thumping. Everyone seemed to be getting into trouble because of me and it was awful. I decided to make a clean breast of things. (What a weird expression. I haven't got a breast yet for a start. And it wasn't even clean because the basin in room 608 was getting so gungy I hadn't felt very much like washing recently.)

'All the Mack jokes – they're mine,' I said.

The Manager and Mrs Hoover both blinked at me.

'You wrote all that revolting rubbish?' said the Manager.

'I thought some of the jokes were quite funny,' I mumbled.

'You children! Vandals! Hooligans!' said the Manager.

'It was just me. Not Pippa. She can't write yet – and even if she could, she quite likes her dad. It's just me that can't stick him. But you can stop telling Mrs Hoover off because, like I said, it was me.'

'Oh Elsa,' said Mrs Hoover. 'He knows I didn't write it, silly. He's cross because I can't clean it all off. Only I keep telling him, that felt-tip just won't budge even though I scrub and scrub.'

'I never see you scrubbing. The hotel is a disgrace. No wonder we have television crews traipsing in here making trouble. If I'm reported to the authorities it will be all your fault.'

'If you get reported to the authorities it'll be because you run a lousy hotel,' said Mrs Hoover. 'How can I possibly hope to keep a huge place like this anywhere near up to standard? Why don't you employ more staff?'

'I'll be employing one less member of staff if you don't watch your tongue,' said the Manager.

'All right then. That suits me. You can stick your stupid job,' said Mrs Hoover, whipping off her overall and throwing it right in his face.

Then she turned on her heel and flounced straight out of his office. I decided it wasn't quite the right time to plead Naomi's case to the Manager. I ran after Mrs Hoover instead.

'Oh gosh, have you really lost your job now? And it's my fault because I did all the scribbling on the walls,' I wailed. 'Oh Mrs Hoover, I'm so sorry!'

'Mrs Whoosit?' said Mrs Hoover. 'Here, is that what you kids call me? Well, don't you fret yourself, pet. I've had it up to here hoovering for that dreadful man. I'll get another cleaning job, they're not that hard to come by even nowadays.'

But I couldn't be absolutely sure she was telling the truth. I wished I was as little as Pippa so she could pick me up and give me a big hug to reassure me. I felt little inside. And stupid. And sad. And sorry.

I was extra loud and noisy and bouncy and bossy at school to try to make myself feel big again. It didn't work. I kept telling jokes to Funny-Face and he kept laughing, but Mrs Fisher was frowning and she made us stay in at playtime and write out I MUST LEARN TO BEHAVE PROPERLY IN THE CLASSROOM fifty times.

Funny-Face is not very good at writing. His words wobble up over the line and slide down below it. His spelling's a bit wobbly too. He missed out one of the 's's in classroom. Mrs Fisher pointed this out huffily. I was scared she might make him do it all over again, so I tried to lighten things a little.

'Why can't you remember there are two 's's in class?' she said crossly. 'I've told you enough times.'

'Which 's' did he leave out this time, Mrs Fisher?' I said.

It was a joke. A bit of a feeble one, but a joke all the same. Only Mrs Fisher just thought I was being cheeky.

Do you know what happened? We had to stay in at lunchtime too. Funny-Face had to write out CLASSROOM another fifty times, and I had to write out a fresh fifty: I MUST LEARN NOT TO BE CHEEKY IN THE CLASSROOM.

'That's silly, anyway,' I muttered. 'That sounds like I can be cheeky in the hall and cheeky in the corridors and cheeky in the toilets and cheeky all over the place. And I wasn't blooming cheeky to start with. I was just joking.'

'You and your
@!+!@ jokes!'
said Funny-Face,
laboriously drawing 's's.

'Hey, don't be like that. Listen, this boy was kept in at lunchtime just like us and his teacher said he had to write out this sentence of not less than fifty words, right? So do you know what he wrote?'

'No, and I don't care,' said Funny-Face. 'Here, I've got all these poxy 's's in the right place, haven't I?'

'Yes. Though hang on, you've started to miss out your 'o's now. There are two in classroom. Like us two in this classroom. But listen to the punchline bit of my joke. This boy wrote, "I went to call my cat in for the night so I stood at the door and called: 'Here, kitty, kitty, kitty, kitty, kitty . . . ' " '

'Shut *up*, Elsa.'

'No, I haven't done enough kittys – there are supposed to be fifty. And you've missed out another 'o' there – *and* there.'

'You'll be going O in a minute, when I punch you right in the nose,' Funny-Face growled.

'What do you give a pig with a sore nose? Oinkment,' I said, snorting like a little pig myself because I think that's one of my funnier jokes.

Funny-Face didn't think it funny at all.

'Why don't you shut your cakehole?' he said, and he sounded so menacing I did what he said.

I wished he hadn't used that expression. We still hadn't been allowed to have our dinners and I kept thinking very wistfully of cake. When horrible old Mrs Fisher eventually let us go, we had to squeeze in right at the end of second-sitting dinners, when all the goodies had long since gone. Not one chip left. We had to make do with a salad, and no-one ever chooses bunny food from choice. I know some excellent bunny jokes but I decided it might be better to keep them in their burrow in my head. Funny-Face still didn't look ready for mirth as he chomped his way morosely through his lettuce.

We had a new teacher in the hall in the afternoon to take us for singing. It was a relief to be free of the Fishy-Eye and I was all set to sing my cares away. I didn't know many of the songs but I've always been good at improvising. So I threw back my head and let rip. But the teacher stopped playing the piano. Her face was all screwed up as if she had a terrible headache.

'Who is making that . . . noise?' she asked.

We stared at her. What did she mean? We were all making a noise. We were singing.

Only she didn't seem to appreciate that. She made us start again, this time without the piano. I decided not to let this faze me. I sang out joyfully. The teacher shuddered.

'You!' she said, pointing.

I peered round. No, it wasn't anyone else. She was pointing at me.

'Yes, you. The little bed-and-breakfast girl.'

The other children around me sniggered. I

felt my face start to burn, like the Royal Hotel's toast.

'Could you try not to sing so loudly, please?' said the teacher.

'Why?' I said, astonished.

'Because you're singing rather flat, dear. And completely out of tune. In fact, it might be better if you didn't sing at all, even softly. How about just nodding your head in time to the music?'

The other kids collapsed, nudging each other and tittering.

'Some stage star, eh! She can't even sing in tune,' they hissed.

I had to spend the whole singing lesson with my mouth shut, nid-nodding away like Little Noddy. I didn't feel much like making a noise after that. I hardly said anything on the way home from school. Funny-Face kept having a go at me, but I didn't respond.

'What's up, Elsa?' said Naomi, putting her arm round me. 'Here, I'm sorry my mum got mad at you. It wasn't really fair for her to pick on you.'

'Oh, I don't know. That's what everyone does. Pick on me,' I said gloomily.

'Hey, don't be like that. You're always so cheerful. I can't bear it when you're all sad. Tell us a joke, go on.'

But for the first time in my life I didn't even feel like telling jokes. Mum gave me a big hug when I went up to room 608. She sent Mack out for a special Kentucky chicken tea.

'To make up for last night, lovie,' said Mum. 'Sorry about that. And Mack's sorry he got snappy too. He's feeling better now.'

Mack might be feeling better, Mum might be feeling better. I didn't feel better at all.

I normally love Kentucky chicken take-aways. I like to sit cross-legged on the floor with Pippa and kid on we're American pioneers like in *Little House on the Prairie*, and we're eating a chicken our Pa has raised and there are prowling bears outside who can smell it cooking but we're safe inside our little log cabin.

'Play our game,' Pippa commanded, but somehow I couldn't make it work.

I usually finish off the game by pretending Hank is a baby bear cub and we all feed him bits of chicken (Hank loves this game too) and then we have a jolly sing-song. But now I didn't feel I ever wanted to sing again.

I didn't want to say anything.

I didn't want to tell jokes.

I didn't want to be me.

328

'Do try and cheer up, Elsa,' said Mum. 'Come on, you're going to have to go to bed if you sulk around the room like this.'

'I don't care,' I said.

So I went to bed really early, before Pippa – even before Hank. Of course it was difficult to get to sleep when the light was on and the telly was loud and there were two and a half people and a baby still racketing round the room, but I put my head way down under the covers and curled up in a little ball with my hands over my ears.

When I woke up I couldn't hear anything even when I took my hands away. I stuck my head out the covers. I could hardly see anything either in the dark. It seemed like the middle of the night.

And yet . . . someone was cooking supper somewhere. I could smell chips. People sometimes stayed up really late and made midnight snacks. I licked my lips. I hadn't eaten all my Kentucky chicken because I'd felt so fed up. I could do with a little snack now myself.

I wondered who was cooking in the kitchen. I'd got to know most of our sixth floor by now. Most of them were quite matey with me. I wondered if they'd consider sharing a chip or two.

I eased myself out of bed. Pippa mumbled

something in her sleep, but didn't wake up. I
picked my way across the crowded floor, tripping over Pippa's My Little Pony and stepping
straight into a Kentucky chicken carton, but
eventually reached the door. I opened it very
slowly so that it wouldn't make any noise and
crept outside into the corridor. Then I stood
still, puzzled. There was a much stronger smell
now. And there was a strange flickering light
coming from right down the end, in the
kitchen. And smoke. You don't get smoke without . . . FIRE!

We Nearly Have Our Chips!

For just one second I stood still, staring. And then I threw back my head and gave a great lion roar.

'FIRE!' I shouted. 'FIRE FIRE FIRE!'

I banged on room 612, I banged on room 611, I banged on room 610, I banged on room 609, charging wildly back down the corridor and bellowing all the while.

'FIRE FIRE FIRE FIRE FIRE FIRE FIRE FIRE FIRE!'

I shouted so long and so loud it felt as if there was a fire in my own head, red and roaring. And then I got to room 608 and I went hurtling inside, screaming and shouting as I snapped on the light.

'FIRE!' I flew to Mum and shook her shoulder hard. Mack propped himself up on one elbow, his eyes bleary. 'Shut that racket!' he mumbled.

'I can't! There's a fire along in the kitchen. Oh, quick, quick, Mum, wake up! Pippa, get up, come on, out of bed.'

Mum sat up, shaking her head, still half-asleep. It was Mack who suddenly shot straight out, grabbing Hank from one bed, Pippa from the other.

'It's OK, Elsa. I'll get them out. You wake the others along the corridor,' he said, busy and brisk.

'Oh good lord, what are we going to do?' Mum said, stumbling out of bed, frantic. 'Quick kids, get dressed as soon as you can – I'll do Hank.'

'No, no, there's no time. We've just got to get out,' said Mack. 'No clothes, no toys, no messing about – OUT!'

'Baby Pillow!' Pippa yelled, struggling, but Mack held her tight.

'I've got him,' I said, snatching Baby Pillow from Pippa's bed.

Then I went charging down the corridor, calling, 'FIRE FIRE FIRE!' all over again.

The smoke was stronger now, and I could hear this awful crackling sound down the corridor. One of the men went running towards the kitchen in his pyjamas, but when he got near he slowed down and then backed away.

'Get everyone out!' he shouted. 'The whole kitchen's ablaze. Keep yelling, little kid. Wake them all up, loud as you can.'

I took a huge breath and roared the dreadful warning over and over again. Some people came running out straight away. Others shouted back, and someone started screaming that we were all going to be burnt alive.

'No-one will be burnt alive if you all just stop panicking,' Mack shouted, charging down the corridor, Pippa under one arm, Hank under the other, Mum stumbling along in her nightie behind them. Mack was only wearing his vest and pants and any other time in the world I'd have rolled around laughing, he looked such a sight.

But we all looked sights. People came blundering out of their bedrooms in nighties and pyjamas and T-shirts and underwear. Some were clutching handbags, some had carrier bags, several had shoved their possessions in blankets and were dragging them along the corridor.

'Leave all your bits and bobs behind. Let's just get out down the stairs. Carry the kids. Come on, get cracking!' Mack yelled. He banged his fist against the fire alarm at the end of the corridor and it started ringing.

'You nip down to the fifth floor and get that alarm going too, Elsa!' Mack yelled. 'And keep calling "Fire!" to get that dozy lot woken up properly. Go on, pal, you're doing great.'

I shot off down the stairs and searched for the fifth-floor fire alarm – but it had already been broken weeks ago by some of the boys and no-one had ever got round to mending it. But I wasn't broken. I was in full working order.

'FIRE!' I roared. 'Get up, get out! Come on, wake up! FIRE FIRE FIRE!'

I ran the length of the corridor and back, banging on every door, screeching until my throat was sore. Then I rushed back down the stairs, pushing past sleepy people stumbling in their nightclothes, desperate to find Mum and Pippa and Hank and Mack, wanting to make sure they were safe.

'Elsa! Elsa, where are you? Come here, baby!'

It was Mum, forcing her way back up the stairs, shouting and screaming.

'Oh Elsa!' she cried, and she swooped on me, clutching me as if she could never let me go. 'I thought you were with us – and then I looked back and you weren't there and I had to come back to get you even though Mack kept telling me you were fine and you were just waking everyone up . . . Oh Elsa, lovie, you're safe!'

335

'Of course I'm safe, Mum,' I said, hugging her fiercely. 'But I've got to get cracking down on the fourth floor now. No-one else has got such a good voice as me. Listen. FIRE!'

I nearly knocked Mum over with the force of my voice.

'Goodness! Yes, well, I don't see how anyone can sleep through that. But it's OK, they've got the other fire alarms going now and some of the men are seeing that everyone's getting out. They've rung for the fire engines. So come on now, darling – hang on tight to my hand,' said Mum.

We made our way down the stairs, clinging to each other. There was no smoke down on the lower floors but people were still panicking, surging out and running like mad, pushing and shoving. One little kid fell down but his mum pulled him up again and one of the men popped him up on his shoulders out of harm's way. The stairs seemed to go on for ever, as if we were going down and down right into the middle of the earth, but at last the lino changed to the cord carpeting of the first floor and then even though our feet kept trying to run downwards, we were on the level of the ground floor.

The Manager was there in a posh camel dressing gown, wringing his hands.

'Which one of you crazies set my hotel on fire?' he screamed. 'I'll have the law on you!'

'And we'll have the law on you too, because your fire alarms aren't working properly and we could all have got roasted to a cinder if it wasn't for my kid,' Mack thundered. He was still clutching Pippa in one arm, Hank in another. He turned to me – and for one mad moment I thought he was going to try to pick me up too. 'Yeah, this little kid here! She raised the alarm. She got us all up and out of it. Our Elsa.'

I'm not Mack's Elsa and I never will be – but I didn't really mind him showing off about me all the same.

'That Elsa!'

'Yes, little Elsa – she yelled "Fire!" fit to bust.'

'She was the one who woke us up – that little kid with the loud voice.'

They were all talking about me as we surged outside the hotel on to the pavement. Lots of people came and patted me on the back and said I'd done a grand job, and one man saw I was shivering out in the cold street and wrapped his jumper right round me to keep me warm. Someone had dragged out a whole pile of blankets and the old ladies and little kids got first pick. There weren't enough to go round.

'Come on, Jimmy, you can be a gent too,' said Mack, seizing hold of the Manager and 'helping' him out of his cosy camel dressing gown. He draped it round a shivery Asian granny who nodded and smiled. The Manager was shaking his head and frowning ferociously. He looked even sillier than Mack now, dressed in a pair of silky boxer shorts and nothing else. The bunny receptionist looked a bit bedraggled too without her angora jumper and with her fluffy hair in curlers. Switchboard looked startling in red satin pyjamas – a bit like a large raspberry jelly. Now that everyone was safe out in the street this fire was almost starting to be fun.

Then we heard a distant clanging and a big cheer went up. The fire engines were coming! We all crowded out of their way, and firemen in yellow helmets went rushing into the hotel with all their firefighting equipment. Lots of the kids wanted to go rushing in after them to watch. Funny-Face had to be frogmarched away by his mum, and Simple Simon and Nicky and Neil started their own fire-engine imitations, barging around bumping into people. Even baby Hank cottoned on and started shrieking like a siren.

Several ambulances arrived although no-one had actually been hurt, and the police came too. And guess who else? A television crew. Not the *Children in Crisis* people. These were from one of the news stations. And there were reporters too, running around with notebooks, and photographers flashing away with their cameras although all the people in their underwear started shrieking. Everyone asked how the fire started and who discovered it and someone said 'Elsa' and then someone else echoed them and soon almost everyone was saying 'Elsa Elsa Elsa'.

Me!

People were prodding me, pushing me forwards towards the cameras and the microphones and the notebooks. It was my Moment of Glory.

And do you know what? I can hardly bear to admit it. I came over all shy. I just wanted to duck my head and hide behind my mum.

'Come on now, lovie. Tell us all about it. You were the one who raised the alarm, weren't you? Come on, sweetheart, no need to be shy. It sounds as if you've been very brave,' they said. 'Tell us in your own words exactly what happened.'

I opened my mouth. But no words came out. It was as if I'd used up all my famous voice yelling 'Fire!' so many times.

So someone else started speaking for me. The wrong someone. The someone who really doesn't have anything to do with me. We're not even related. Though now he was acting as if he was my dad and I was his daughter.

'The poor wee girl's still a bit gob-smacked – and no wonder! My, but she did a grand job raising the alarm,' Mack boasted, strutting all around. He was careful to hold in his tummy

all the time the cameras were pointing his way. He couldn't flex his arm muscles properly because he was still carrying Pippa and Hank, but he kept carefully arranging his legs as if he was posing for Mister Universe. He didn't half look a berk. He sounded a right berk too, prattling on and on about his wee Elsa. If I'd had any voice left at all I'd have contradicted him furiously.

Then little Pippa piped up.

'Yes, my sister Elsa's ever so big and brave. She rescued my baby!'

'She rescued the baby?' said the reporters, looking at Hank.

'Yep, she went and got him out of his cot. I was crying and crying because I thought he'd get all burnt up and Dad and Mum wouldn't let me go back for him—'

'They wouldn't go back for the *baby*?' said the reporters, their eyes swivelling from Hank to Mum and Mack.

'Not *our* baby. It's just Pippa's pillow. She calls it her baby,' said Mum quickly. Then she realized the cameras were aiming at her, and she clutched her nightie with one hand and did her best to tidy her hair with the other. 'Don't worry, we made sure we had our baby Hank safe and sound. But certainly if it hadn't been for our Elsa then we could still be in our beds right this minute – charred to cinders,' said Mum dramatically.

'Yes, Elsa banged on our door and woke us all up. We'd be dead if it wasn't for her. She rescued all of us,' said Naomi's mum.

'Me and all *my* babies,' she said, showing them off to the camera.

'Elsa's my best friend,' said Naomi, nodding her head so that her plaits jiggled.

'Elsa's *my* best friend too and she rescued us and all,' said Funny-Face, and then he pulled the funniest face he could manage, all cross-eyes and drooly mouth until his mum gave him a poke.

My mum was giving me a poke too.

'Come on then, pet. Haven't you got anything to say for yourself? All these nice gentlemen want you to say a few words about the fire. Come on, lovie, this is your big chance,' Mum hissed.

I knew it. I swallowed. I wet my lips. I took a deep breath.

'Fire,' I mumbled. It was as if my voice could still only say one thing. I concentrated fiercely, trying to gain control. Fire crackled through my thoughts. My brain suddenly glowed.

'Do you know what happened to the plastic surgeon who got too close to the fire?' I said, in almost my own voice.

'What plastic surgeon? There was a medical man in there? Did he get out OK?' the reporters clamoured.

'He melted!' I said, and fell about laughing.

They blinked at me, missing a beat.

I decided to forge right ahead like a true professional.

'What were the two Spanish firemen called?'

'We haven't got any Spaniards in our team,' said one of the firemen, wiping the sweat from his brow and replacing his helmet.

'OK, but what would they be called? Hosé and Hose B! Do you get it?'

He didn't look very sure. Mum gave me a violent nudge.

'Elsa, stop telling those silly *jokes*!'

But once I got started I couldn't ever seem to stop.

'Why did the fireman wear red trousers?' I paused for a fraction. Everyone was still staring at me oddly. 'His blue ones were at the cleaners!'

'Pack it in, Elsa,' Mack hissed, looking like he wasn't so sure he wanted me to be his wee Elsa after all.

'It's the shock,' said Mum firmly. 'She's just having a funny five minutes.'

'Only she's not being flipping funny,' said Mack.

'Yep, I think we'd better cut the jokes,' said the television man gently.

'I'll try harder,' I said desperately. 'I'll try a new set of jokes, OK? Or I could put on a silly voice . . . ?'

'Why not use your own voice, Elsa? And why do you have to try so hard? Just be yourself. Act natural,' said the television man, chucking me under the chin. 'Let's start again, hmm? Tell us in your own words exactly what happened.'

'But if I just say any old thing, without any jokes, then I'm not funny,' I wailed.

'Who says you've got to be funny?'

'Well, I want to be a comedienne and get to be famous.'

'You don't have to be funny to be famous. And we don't really want people chortling when this goes out on the news. We want to touch the heart. We've got a super story here. You're a great little kid, Elsa. You'll come over really well on television if you just *relax*.'

'It's kind of difficult to act relaxed when you're standing on the pavement in your T-shirt and knickers and a whole bunch of strangers are asking you questions,' I said, sighing.

I wasn't trying to be funny. But the weirdest thing happened. Everyone chuckled appreciatively.

'So what happened, Elsa? You woke up in the middle of the night and . . . ?'

And so I started to tell them exactly what happened. I said I thought the smell was someone cooking chips and I started to get peckish and slipped out of bed to go and beg a few chips for myself. (They laughed again.) Then I told about tripping over Pippa's My Little Pony. (More laughter – and I still hadn't told a single joke!) Then I went on about the fire and dashing up and down the corridor banging on the doors and yelling. (I waited for them to laugh again, but this time they listened spellbound.) The television man asked what I'd yelled and I said 'Fire' and he said that wasn't very loud and *I* said well, I did it a lot louder. And he said show us. So I did. I threw back my head and roared.

'F-I-I-I-I-I-I-I-I-I-I-I-I-I-I-I-I-I-R-E!!!'

That nearly blew them all backwards. Most people had their hands over their ears. Some shook their heads, dazed. Then someone laughed. They all joined in. Someone else cheered. Someone else did too. Lots of cheers. For me. FOR ME!

346

It really was my Moment of Fame. I hadn't blown it after all.

My interview went out on the television. I thought I sounded sort of stupid, but everyone else said it went splendidly. (Well, Mum moaned because her hair was a sight and she didn't have any make-up on, and Mack fussed because they'd cut out most of his bits and he was only shown from the waist up so no-one could see his great hairy legs.) But they didn't cut *any* of my bits.

I might not have made it into the *Children in Crisis* documentary. But guess what. My news interview was repeated later in the year in a special compilation programme called *Children of Courage*. And I got to do another interview with a nice blonde lady with big teeth, and Mum spent some of Mack's betting money on a beautiful new outfit from the Flowerfields Shopping Centre for my special telly appearance. Mum made me try on lots of frilly frocks but they all looked *awful*.

So she gave up and let me choose instead. I wanted black jeans (so they wouldn't show the dirt). Mum bought me a black top too, and tied her red scarf round my neck, and then guess what we found at a car-boot sale? Red cowboy boots! They were a bit big but we stuffed the toes with paper and I looked absolutely great.

The blonde lady with the big teeth loved my outfit too. She said I looked just like a cowboy. I was a bit nervous so without thinking I got launched into a cowboy joke routine.

'Who wears a cowboy hat and spurs and lives under the sea? Billy the Squid!'

She laughed! It wasn't *that* funny, one of my oldest jokes actually, but she laughed and laughed and laughed. She said she loved jokes, the older and cornier the better, and she said I could maybe come on her special show one day and do my own comedy routine !!!!!

We couldn't go back to bed in room 608 when the firemen put the fire out at last. It wasn't all burnt to bits. It was only the kitchen that had cooked itself into little black crumbs. But the whole corridor was thick with smoke and sloshy with water and all the rooms looked as if someone had run amok with giant paint-brushes and vats of black paint. All our stuff was covered in this black treacle, and there was a sharp smell that scratched at your nostrils.

'Sorry, folks. You'll have to stay in temporary accommodation for a few weeks,' said the Chief Fireman, shaking his head.

He looked surprised when all the residents of the Royal gave a hearty cheer. The Manager was prancing about in his silk boxer shorts, pointing out that only a few of the rooms were seriously fire damaged, and that the first few floors were barely affected. There was a lot of rushing around consulting, and eventually it was decided that only the people living on the top two floors need be evacuated.

Us sixth-floor and fifth-floor people hugged and danced and shouted. All the other residents booed and argued and complained. Naomi and I had a big hug because she's on the fifth floor so she could come too. Then Funny-Face came and clapped hands with me because though he's on the fourth floor their room is right below the burnt kitchen and water had swirled right down through the room underneath and was dripping through to them, so they couldn't stay either.

We were all ferried off in police cars and coaches to this church hall, where several big bossy ladies with cardigans over their nighties handed out blankets and pillows and sleeping bags. They gave us paper cups of hot soup too – which we needed, because the church hall was freezing. The floor was slippery lino and fun to skid across in your socks, but not exactly cosy or comfy when we settled down to go to sleep. I didn't exactly rate bed number eight – and it soon got crowded because Pippa unzipped my sleeping bag and stuck herself in too. She kept

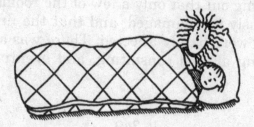

having nightmares and twitching and I had to keep waking her up and dragging her off to the toilet because I was all too aware of what would happen if I didn't.

There was only one toilet and there were queues for it all night long. It was worse in the morning. There was only the one small wash-basin too, and most people didn't have their toothbrushes or flannels or towels anyway.

'I don't know why we were flipping cheering last night,' said Mum, trying to wipe round Hank's sticky face with a damp hankie. 'Compared with this draughty old dump the Royal is practically a palace.'

'We can't stay here,' said Mack, sitting up and scratching. 'I'm going right down that Housing Department first thing.'

'Oh yeah?' said Mum, looking at him. 'You're walking down the road in your underpants, right? Don't forget you haven't even got any trousers any more. And look at me! This is all I've got – the old nightie that I'm wearing. All my clothes, all my make-up, my crinoline-lady ornament . . . all gone! Even if they're not ruined by that smoke then someone will be bound to nick them before I can get back to claim them.' She started to cry so I went and put my arms round her.

'Don't cry, Mum,' I said, hugging her tight.

'You've still got us.'

Mum snuffled a bit but then hugged me back.

'Yes, that's right, Elsa. I've still got my family. My Mack. My baby. My little girl. And my special big girl.'

The special big girl went a bit snuffly herself then. I was glad that Funny-Face in the next row of sleeping bags was still fast asleep or he might have jeered. He looked oddly little, snuggled up under the blanket. And he sucked his thumb and all!

More big bossy ladies breezed into the hall and started heating up a big urn of tea. They had lots of packets of biscuits too. I helped hand them round to everyone. We could have seconds and even thirds. A Bourbon, a short-bread finger and a chocolate Hob Nob make quite a good breakfast.

Then the ladies started dragging in great black plastic sacks crammed with clothes.

'Come and help yourselves! There should be enough for a new outfit for everyone.'

'Oh, big deal,' Mum grumbled. 'It's just tatty old junk left over from jumbles. I'm not wearing anyone's old Crimplene cast-offs.'

She watched Funny-Face's mum trying to squeeze herself into a tight black skirt.

'She's wasting her time. She'll never get that

over her big bum,' Mum mumbled, and when Funny-Face's mum had to give up the attempt, Mum darted out and snatched the skirt herself.

'There! I thought so! That's a Betty Barclay skirt. I've seen them on sale in Flowerfields. Hey, look, does it fit?' Mum pulled it up over her narrow hips and stood preening. 'I wonder if there's a jacket to go with it, eh?'

Mum started skimming her way through the plastic sacks and came up with all sorts of goodies – even a pair of patent high heels her exact size. She had more trouble finding stuff for Mack, considering the only size he takes is *out*-size. She found a jumper that could just about go round him, but the biggest trousers could barely do up and the legs ended way above his ankles. Hank was a bit of a problem too – there were heaps of baby clothes, but he's such a *big* baby that the average one-year-old's sleeping suit came unpopped every time he breathed out and bent him up double into the bargain. Pippa was fine, fitting all the little frocks a treat, but I looked such a fool in the only one my size that Mum threw it back in the pile. (Naomi tried it on instead and looked gorgeous, but then she always does.) Funny-Face was delving in a sack of boys' clothes so I had a sift through too and found some jeans and a jumper and a really great baseball bomber jacket with a picture of a lion on the back!

'Well, we're all kitted out like a dog's dinner, but we've still got no place to go,' said Mack.

But he was wrong.

Oh, you'll never guess where we ended up! Someone from the Social and the man from the Housing Office came round to the church hall to tell us. We were all going to be temporarily accommodated in another hotel. Not a special bed-and-breakfast DHS dumping ground. A *real* hotel. The Star Hotel. With stars after its name.

When we stepped through those starry glass doors it was like finding fairyland. There were soft sofas all over the reception area, and thick red carpet and flowers in great vases, and a huge chandelier sparkled from the ceiling. All us lot from the Oyal Htl crowded into the reception area, and Mum and Mack and Naomi's mum and Funny-Face's mum and dad and all the other grown-ups sprawled on the sofas while we all ran round and round the red carpet and up and down the wide staircase and rang all the bells on the lifts.

The Star Manager came out of his office to meet us. He didn't look terribly thrilled to see us, but he shook us all by the hand, even the littlest stickiest kid, and welcomed us to the Star Hotel. Then there was a lot of hoo-ha and argy-bargy about rooms, with the Manager and his chief receptionist going into a huddle. This receptionist was dark instead of blonde, and fierce instead of fluffy, but she also had long pointy fingernails and she started to tap them very impatiently indeed. But at last it was all sorted out and she handed all of us little cards instead of keys.

We were in suite 13. It might be an unlucky number for some people, but it was lucky lucky lucky for us.

Note I said suite, not room. As we shot up one floor in the lift and padded along the thickly carpeted corridor, Pippa licked her lips hopefully, thinking we were going to be given a sweety sweet. Even I didn't twig what suite really meant.

Suite 13 wasn't just one room. It was a set of

three rooms, just like a little flat. Only there was nothing little about suite 13. It was really big – and *beautiful*. The main room was blue, with deeper blue velvet curtains and a dark blue coverlet on the huge bed. There was a painting on the wall of a boy in a blue velvet suit and a blue glass vase on the bedside table filled with little blue pretendy rosebuds. There was a dressing table with swivel mirrors so you could see the back of your head, and a blue leather folder containing notepaper and envelopes, and a blue felt-tip pen patterned with stars. There was a big television too – a colour one – and it even had Sky!

There was a bathroom leading off this main room. It was blue too, with a blue bath, blue

basin, even a blue loo. They all shone like the sea they were so sparkly clean. Laid out on the gleaming tiled shelf were little blue bottles of shampoo and bath gel and tiny cakes of forget-me-not soap. Mum sniffed them rapturously, her eyes shining.

Mack kicked his shoes off and lay on the big bed, Hank sitting astride his tummy. The bed was so big that even Mack could fit right inside it, and his feet wouldn't stick out at the end. I thought we might *all* have to fit inside it, because it was the only bed in the room.

Then I saw another door and opened it. There was another bedroom, with three single beds, three little beside tables, and three little wooden chairs with carved hearts and painted roses. It was just like the three bears fairy

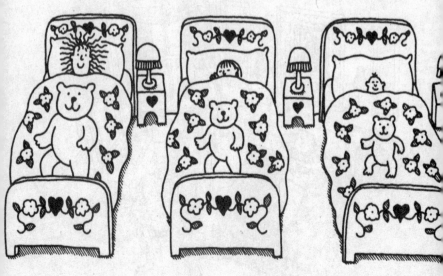

story – and there were bears on the duvets too, and a painting of Goldilocks up on the wall. The carpet and wallpaper were pale blue but the ceiling was a deep navy, with stars scattered all over it. That night when I slept in my wonderful, soft, splendid bed number nine I could still see the stars, even with the light switched off. They glowed luminously in the dark, my own magic midnight stars. I didn't want to sleep, just in case this was all a wonderful dream and when I woke up I'd be back in the grotty old Oyal Htl.

But it wasn't a dream at all. I woke up early and lay luxuriating in my bed and then I crept into Mum and Mack's room. They were all cuddled up together, looking friendly even though they were fast asleep. I sat down at the dressing table and practised a few funny faces and then I took a piece of paper and the felt-tip pen and wrote letters to all my friends.

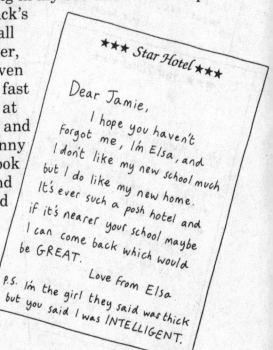

★★★ Star Hotel ★★★

Dear Jamie,

I hope you haven't forgot me, I'm Elsa, and I don't like my new school much but I do like my new home. It's ever such a posh hotel and if it's nearer your school maybe I can come back which would be GREAT.

Love from Elsa

P.S. I'm the girl they said was thick but you said I was INTELLIGENT.

★★★ Star Hotel ★★★

Dear Mrs Hoover, Sorry
Mrs Macpherson,

Hey, this hotel is
HEAPS better than the Royal.
Why don't you come and work
here? I bet you'd like it and
I'd give you a hand. The walls
have all got fancy paper so
no-one ever scribbles on them.

Love from Elsa

★★★ Star Hotel ★★★

Dear Naomi,

Isn't it super here. My
bedroom's got stars on the
ceiling, has yours? I hope we
don't have to go back to the
Royal for ages and ages.

See you at breakfast.

Love from your friend Elsa

× × ×

★★★ Star Hotel ★★★

Dear Funny-Face,

There are lots of bushes
and trees and stuff at the
end of the Star Hotel garden
so maybe we could make
a camp ???

See you.

Elsa

★★★ Star Hotel ★★★

Dear Pippa,

I will read you this letter
seeing as you can't read
yet yourself. It is from me,
Elsa, and it's just to say
HELLO and we'll play lots
today.

Love from your big sister
Elsa

× × × × × × × × × × × ×

★★★ *Star Hotel* ★★★

Dear Hank,
     Hello Big Baby
Love from your big
sister Elsa

X X X

★★★ *Star Hotel* ★★★

Dear Mum,
     It's so lovely here I don't
think you'll ever be sad
or cross ever again, eh?
     Lots and lots of love
          from Elsa

X X X X X X X X X X X X

★★★ *Star Hotel* ★★★

Dear Mack,
     Och Aye the Noo.
That's all the Scotch
     I know.
               From Elsa

★★★ *Star Hotel* ★★★

Dear Elsa,
     I am having a lovely time
here. I have been writing
lots and lots of letters. I even
wrote one to the warthog !!!
     But I am too happy to hate
anyone and there are stars
on my ceiling and I have
stars in my eyes because it
is so super here at the Star
Hotel.
          Love and X X X
               from Elsa

There! I used up all the notepaper and gave myself a big appetite for breakfast.

Ooooh the breakfast! You have it in a lovely room with a dark pink swirly carpet and pink fuzzy paper on the walls and rose-pink cloths on the tables. You sit at a table and spread a rose-pink napkin on your lap and a waitress in a black frock and a white apron comes and asks what you want to drink. Then you go and help yourself to whatever you want to eat from the breakfast bar. You can have whatever you want. Lots and lots and lots of it.

Even Mum had more breakfast than usual. She had freshly squeezed orange juice and black coffee and toast and butter and marmalade.

Mack had tea and a bowl of porridge because he's Scottish and then he had a big plate of

bacon and egg and mushroom and fried potatoes and more bacon because that's his
favourite, and he tucked the extra bacon into
toast to make a bacon butty.

Pippa didn't copy me! She chose all by herself. Apple juice and Cocoa Pops and milk and
a soft white roll and butter and honey.

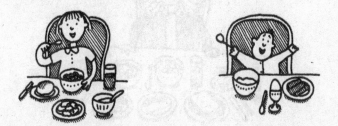

Hank had hot milk and a little bowl of
porridge like his dad and a runny egg and tiny
toast soldiers. He loved this breakfast and
wanted to wave his arms about to show his
appreciation and he dropped a few crumbs
(more than a few, actually) on the carpet, but
no-one seemed to mind and the waitress tickled him under the chin and said he was a
chubby little cherub!

Mum and Mack and Pippa and Hank all
knew exactly what they wanted for breakfast.
I was the one who simply couldn't decide
because it all looked so delicious. So guess

what. I had almost all of it.

I had milky tea and cranberry juice and cornflakes sprinkled with rainbow sugar and then muesli with extra sultanas and apple

rings and then scrambled egg on toast with tomato sauce and then sausages stuck in a long roll to make a hot dog and then a big jammy Danish pastry and I ate it all up, every little bit. It was the best breakfast ever.

What with the cranberry juice and the cherry jam in the pastry I ended up looking like Dracula. And that reminded me of a Dracula breakfast joke and that got me started.

I told jokes to Mum and Mack and Pippa and Hank and I shouted them to Naomi and Funny-Face across the tables and I tried them out on our waitress too because she seemed friendly and she said I was a proper caution. Do you want to hear a small sample?

What does Dracula like for breakfast?
Readyneck.

What do ghosts like for breakfast?
Dreaded wheat.

What do cannibals like for breakfast?
Buttered host.

What do Frenchmen eat for breakfast?
Huit heures bix.

How would a cannibal describe a man in a hammock?
Breakfast in bed.

What happens when a baby eats Rice Krispies?
It goes snap, crackle and poop.

I *must* stop rabbiting on like this. Well. Just one more.

What do you get if you pour boiling water down a rabbit hole?

365

Hot cross bunnies!

I'm not hot. I feel super-cool.
I'm not cross. I'm happy happy happy.
I'm not a bunny. I'm Elsa and I roar like a lion.

Hey, what do you get if you cross a lion with a parrot?
I don't know, but if he says 'Pretty Polly' you'd better
                    SMILE

☆ CHECK OUT ☆ JACQUELINE WILSON'S OFFICIAL WEBSITE!

You'll find lots of fun stuff including games and amazing competitions. You can even customise your own page and start an online diary!

You'll find out all about Jacqueline in her monthly diary and tour blogs, as well as seeing her replies to fan mail. You can also chat to other fans on the message boards.

Join in today at
www.jacquelinewilson.co.uk

And to view the exciting book trailers including *Lily Alone*, *Sapphire Battersea* and *The Worst Thing About My Sister*, visit Jacqueline's official YouTube channel at
www.youtube.com/jacquelinewilson.tv